"Rafe."

Carin cleared her throat. Fear danced along her spine, but that was silly. What was there to be afraid of?

"You seem surprised to see me, Carin."

"Yes. I—I am. What—what are you doing here?"

"Why, *querida,* I am here to see you, of course." He glanced at the sleeping infant in his arms. "And to see your daughter."

Carin's gaze flew to the baby, then to him. "What are you doing with my baby?"

"Don't you mean, what am I doing with *our* baby? That seems to be the consensus, *querida,* that this child is mine."

SANDRA MARTON is an author who used to tell stories to her dolls when she was a little girl. Today, readers around the world fall in love with her sexy, dynamic heroes and outspoken, independent heroines. Her books have topped bestseller lists and won many awards. Sandra loves dressing up for a night out with her husband as much as she loves putting on her hiking boots for a walk in a south-western desert or a north-eastern forest. You can write to her (SASE) at P.O. Box 295, Storrs, Connecticut, USA. *The Alvares Bride* is the sixth book in her well-loved miniseries THE BARONS.

Look out for Samantha's story expected Spring 2002!

Sandra Marton

THE ALVARES BRIDE

THE BARONS

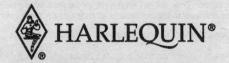

HARLEQUIN®

TORONTO • NEW YORK • LONDON
AMSTERDAM • PARIS • SYDNEY • HAMBURG
STOCKHOLM • ATHENS • TOKYO • MILAN • MADRID
PRAGUE • WARSAW • BUDAPEST • AUCKLAND

ISBN 0-373-12202-0

THE ALVARES BRIDE

First North American Publication 2001.

This edition published by arrangement with Harlequin Books S.A.

® and TM are trademarks of the publisher. Trademarks indicated with
® are registered in the United States Patent and Trademark Office, the
Canadian Trade Marks Office and in other countries.

Visit us at www.eHarlequin.com

Printed in U.S.A.

CHAPTER ONE

New York City
Saturday, May 4

CARIN BREWSTER clutched her sister's hand and wondered how the human race had managed to survive if every woman who'd ever borne a child had to go through agony like this.

She groaned as another contraction racked her body.

"That's it," Amanda Brewster al Rashid said. "Push, Carin. Push!"

"I—*am*—pushing," Carin panted.

"Mom's on the way. She should be here soon."

"Great." Carin bit down on her lip. "She can tell me she knows the right way to—ohhh, God!"

"Oh, sweetie." Amanda leaned closer. "Don't you think it's time you told me who—"

"No!"

"I don't understand you, Carin! He's the father of your child."

"Don't—need—him."

"But he has the right to know what's happening!"

"He—has—no—rights."

Carin grimaced with pain. What rights did a man have, when he was almost a stranger? None. None at all. Some of the decisions she'd made over the past months had been difficult. Whether to keep her baby. Whether to turn to her family for help. But deciding not to tell Rafe Alvares that

5

he'd made her pregnant had been easy. He didn't give a damn about her; why would he want to know? Why would a man who'd spent an hour in her bed and never tried to contact her again, want to know he was going to be a father?

The contraction subsided. Carin fell back against the pillows.

"He's not important. The baby's mine. I'm all that she'll need. Just…" She groaned, arched from the bed. "…just me."

"That's crazy." Amanda wiped her sister's forehead with a cool washcloth. "Please, Sis, tell me his name. Let me call him. Is it Frank?"

"No!" Carin grasped Amanda's hand more tightly. "It's not Frank. And I'm not going to tell you anything else. Mandy, you said you wouldn't do this. You promised. You said—"

"Madame al Rashid? Excuse me, please, but I need to speak with your sister."

Carin turned her head. Sweat had run into her eyes and her vision was blurry but she could see Amanda step back to make room for Dr. Ronald.

He sat down next to her and took her hand.

"How're you doing, Carin?"

"I'm…" She hesitated. "I'm fine."

The doctor smiled. "You're one tough cookie, that's for sure. But we think you've been at this long enough."

Somehow, she managed a weak grin. "Try telling that to this baby."

"That's exactly what I'm going to do. We've decided to take you down the hall and get this kid into the world. How's that sound?"

"Will it hurt my—"

Another contraction gripped her body. Carin groaned and

the doctor squeezed her hand. "No. On the contrary. It'll conserve energy for the two of you. It's the best thing to do, I promise."

The doctor rose to his feet and moved aside as two white-coated attendants came towards the bed.

"Don't you worry, missus," one of them said. "You'll be holding that baby of yours before you know it."

I'm not a missus, Carin thought, but everything was happening quickly now. Gentle hands lifted her; Amanda hurried alongside as she was rolled down the long corridor, her eyes fixed on the endless lights that shone from the ceiling. A pair of doors swooshed open just ahead, and her sister bent down and kissed her damp forehead.

"Hey," she whispered.

"Hey," Carin said softly.

"I love you, Sis."

"Me, too," Carin said, and then she was through the door and in a room with white tile walls, staring up at a light as bright as the sun.

"Just relax, Ms. Brewster," a voice told her, and there was a sudden burning sensation in her arm, where an IV needle already snaked under her skin.

"Here we go," her doctor said, and Carin spun away.

Minutes passed, or maybe an hour; she couldn't tell. She was drifting on a sea of soft clouds as she waited for the sound of her baby's cry, but the doctor saying something in a sharp tone and then other voices joined in, calling out numbers, demanding five units of blood, stat.

Carin forced her eyes open. The light was blinding now. A nurse bent over her and she tried to speak because suddenly she wanted someone to know what had happened, that her child had a father, that she could not forget him or the hour she had spent in his arms...

And then everything faded to black, she was tumbling

down a deep, deep tunnel, and suddenly, it was a hot August night instead of a warm Spring morning. She was at Espada, not in a hospital, and her life was about to change, forever...

He was tall and good-looking, and he'd been watching her ever since she'd entered the room.

His name, Carin figured, had to be Raphael Alvares.

'The Latin Lover,' she'd dubbed him, when Amanda had done everything but handstands to convince her she just had to meet the man.

"He's a friend of Nick's, and he's here to buy horses from Jonas," Amanda had confided as she sat in the guest room, watching Carin brush out her long, dark hair. "And, of course, Mother invited him to stay for the weekend." She grinned. "Matchmaker, matchmaker," she began singing, and Carin covered her ears.

"Stop!" She sighed with resignation. Well, it wasn't a surprise. She should have known her mother wouldn't give up the idea of marrying off her remaining two daughters. Samantha was safely out of range, flitting around Europe somewhere, which left Marta free to concentrate all her efforts on Carin, even though she'd vowed never to get involved with a man again. Marta had no way of knowing that but even if she had, it wouldn't have stopped her.

"He's gorgeous," Amanda gushed, "and rich, and incredibly yummy. Well, not quite as yummy as my Nicholas, of course, but he's really something special."

"How nice for him," Carin said politely.

"His name is Raphael Alvares. Isn't that sexy?"

"Actually," Carin said, even more politely, "I think it's Spanish."

Amanda had giggled. "Brazilian," she'd replied, in an

exaggerated accent, "wheech, my 'usband says, means zat he is zee *Senhor* Alvares, and not zee *señor*."

She'd laughed, and Carin had grinned, and that had been that.

Carin had half expected her sister to drag her off to meet the man right there and then, but Amanda had apparently decided on a more subtle approach.

Instead of pointing Carin at Raphael Alvares, she'd pointed him at Carin.

At least, she must have, because the man who had to be the *senhor* from Brazil kept staring at her. Once in a while he smiled, as he was doing now. She smiled back, because it was the polite thing to do, but he wasn't her type. No man was her type, anymore. To put it more accurately, she wasn't the type for any man. Not now, maybe not for the rest of her life.

She lifted her wine goblet to her lips and took a drink so that she wouldn't have to go on smiling when smiling was the last thing she felt like doing, and turned her back on the *senhor*.

The wine went down smoothly, maybe because it was her second, or was it her third, glass. She didn't drink red wine, as a rule, not even one like this which had, undoubtedly, come from the Espada wine cellar and probably cost almost as much as she'd paid in rent on her first apartment in New York six years ago, but the first waiter she'd seen had been carrying a tray filled with glasses of red wine.

"Beggars can't be choosers," she'd quipped, and snatched one from him.

It was for false courage, she knew, but then, this was a weekend that called for it. Screamed for it, she thought, and drank more of the wine.

Her mother thought she was here because of the anniversary party for Tyler and Caitlin. At least, she was pretending she thought that was the reason, which was sweet of her.

"I can't come, Mother," Carin had said, when Marta phoned.

She'd been genuinely regretful, too. The gathering of the clan, all the Barons and Kincaids and al Rashids, was always a noisy, impossible, exciting event, and then there were all those adorable babies her stepbrothers' wives and her very own sister were popping out, as if "fecundity" were their middle names.

"I wish I could," she'd added, "but I'll be at a wedding that weekend."

That, of course, had all changed.

Latin Lover was staring again. She could almost feel his eyes on the exposed nape of her neck.

"Wear your hair up," Amanda had urged, and she'd done it, except now her neck felt naked, which was dumb, but there was something about the way Raphael Alvares kept looking at her that made her feel uncomfortable. She thought about turning around and staring back but that might give him the wrong idea, which would be stupid. And she'd had quite enough of being stupid for a while.

Instead, she took another sip of the wine. It didn't taste as bad as it had, at first. Well, who knew? Maybe red wine had to grow on a person, the way extended families did.

The idea was so silly it made her giggle. A woman standing nearby looked around.

"Nothing," Carin said, when the woman smiled and raised her eyebrows questioningly. "I just thought of something, and…"

The woman nodded and turned away. Carin buried her face in her glass again and drank more deeply.

Yes, even if she wasn't mingling, as Amanda had urged

her to do, maybe it was a good idea that she'd come tonight, even if the reason sounded too ridiculous for words.

The man she'd been seeing for almost six months had been seeing one of her best friends at the same time he'd been dating her. It was such a clichéd, sad little tale that it would have been quite unremarkable—except for a minor deviation.

He wasn't just dating Iris, he'd become engaged to her. The wedding date was set, the arrangements all made...and Carin was to be one of the bridesmaids.

"I can't believe I've never met that fiancé of yours," she'd said to Iris once, with a little laugh, and Iris, as ignorant of the truth as Carin, had explained that he traveled a lot.

Carin finished her wine just as she spotted another waiter with a tray of drinks.

"Waiter," she said briskly.

There were no glasses of wine on the tray, only cocktail glasses filled with a colorless liquid and onions or olives impaled on tiny plastic swords.

"Cute," she said, and smiled as she swapped her empty glass for a full one that held an onion and then, because the drink looked small, she shifted her evening bag under her arm and took a second glass that contained an olive.

The waiter lifted an eyebrow.

"Thank you," Carin said, as if she drank two-fisted every day of her life. She took a sip of the glass that held the onion. "Wow," she whispered, and took a second sip.

It was true. Frank had, in fact, traveled a lot. What neither she nor Iris knew was that the traveling he did was mostly between their two apartments. Thinking back, remembering how naive—no, how stupid—she'd been she almost laughed.

A month ago, it had all come apart. Frank must have

realized he couldn't keep up the act much longer, not with things like the rehearsal dinner and his marriage vows staring him in the face. So he'd phoned one evening, sounding nervous, and said he had to see her right away; he had to tell her something important.

Carin had hurried down to the corner wine shop, bought a bottle of champagne and popped it into the fridge. He was going to propose, she'd thought giddily...

Instead, he'd told her that he'd trapped himself in a nightmare. He had, he said, become engaged to another woman. And while she was staring at him in horror, trying to digest that news, he'd told her who the woman was.

"You're joking," Carin had said, when she could finally choke out a coherent sentence.

Frank had shrugged, grinned sheepishly—grinned, of all things—and that was when she'd lost it, when she'd gone from gasping to shrieking and screaming. She'd thrown things at him—a vase, the waiting wine bucket—and he'd run for the door.

Carin took a deep breath, raised her glass to her lips and drank down half of the martini.

She'd survived, even managed to put it all in perspective. Frank was no great loss; a man like that, one who couldn't remain faithful, was not a man she'd want for a husband. All she had to do was get through the wedding that loomed ahead—the wedding between the woman who'd been her friend and the man who'd been her lover—and she'd be fine. She wouldn't attend the wedding, of course, but that didn't mean she'd mope.

No, she'd told herself firmly, no moping. No sitting around feeling sorry for herself. She'd order in pizza, drink the bottle of champagne she'd put in the fridge that horrid evening. To hell with Frank. Iris could have him.

Everything was fine, or almost fine, until an invitation to

the wedding arrived along with a note from Iris asking, very politely, if she'd mind passing along her bridesmaid's gown to the girl who'd be taking her place.

Carin had ripped the note and the invitation into tiny pieces, stuffed them back into their envelope and mailed it to the happy couple. Then, because it was time to admit she'd never get through the wedding weekend alone without either crying or screaming or maybe even going to the wedding and standing up to make a public announcement when the minister got to the part where he'd ask if anyone present knew a reason the marriage shouldn't take place, she'd phoned Marta and said, as gaily as she could, that there'd been a change in plans and she'd be flying in for the party, after all.

"With Frank?" her mother had asked and when Carin said no, no, he wouldn't be coming, Marta had said "oh" in a tone that spoke volumes. If she knew more now, if Amanda had told her anything, she hadn't let on, except to hug Carin tightly when she arrived and whisper, "I never liked him, anyway."

Carin sighed.

Nobody had liked Frank, it was turning out. Not her secretary, who'd wanted to kill him almost as much as Carin. Not Amanda, not Nicholas, not anybody with half a brain—except her. She'd been so dumb...

"Canapés, miss?"

Carin looked up, smiled at the white-gloved waiter, put the empty martini glass on a table and plucked a tiny puff pastry from the tray.

"What is it?" she asked.

"Lobster, I believe, miss."

Lobster, indeed, and decadently delicious, Carin thought as she popped the little hors d'oeuvre into her mouth and crunched down. All that it needed was another swallow of whatever was in the glass with the onion to make it perfect...except, the glass was empty.

How had that happened? Well, it was a problem easily solved. She put the empty glass beside the other and set off through the crowded room in search of a drink.

"Mizz?"

The voice was masculine, heavily accented, and right behind her. She took a deep breath, pasted a smile to her lips and turned around. As she'd expected, it was the Brazilian Bombshell.

Up close, he wasn't quite so good-looking. His jaw was a little weak, his nose a little long. Actually, he looked a lot like Frank.

"Mizz," he said again, and took her hand. He bent over it, brought it to his lips, planted a damp kiss on her skin. Carin snatched her hand back and fought against the almost overwhelming desire to wipe it on her gown.

"Hello," she said as pleasantly as she could.

"Hello," he said, and smiled so broadly she could see a filling in his molar. "I ask who is the beautiful lady with the black hair and the green eyes and I am tell she is Carin Brewster, yes?"

"Yes," Carin said. Was this what a Portuguese accent sounded like? "I mean, thank you for the compliment, *senhor*."

"*Senhor*," he repeated, and laughed. "Is amusing you should call me that, Carin Brewster."

"Well, I know my pronunciation isn't very good, but—"

She babbled her way through a conversation that made little sense. The Latin Lover spoke poor English and she spoke no Portuguese. Besides, she really didn't want to talk with him. She didn't want to talk to anybody, especially not a man who reminded her, even slightly, of Frank.

Frank, that no-good rat. That scum-sucking bottom

crawler. That liar—but then, all men were liars. She'd learned that, early. Her father had lied to her mother. To her, too, each time she'd climbed into his lap and begged him not to go away again.

"This is the last time, angel," he'd say, but that was never the truth.

What was wrong with the Brewster women? Hadn't they learned anything? Their father had lied. From the stories she'd heard, Jonas Baron had turned lying into an art form. Yes, there might be exceptions. She was hopeful about her stepbrothers, and about Amanda's new husband but still, as a rule—

"...a funny joke, yes?"

Carin nodded her head and laughed mechanically. Whatever joke the *senhor* had told, it couldn't be half as funny as the one she'd thought of.

Question: How do you know a man is lying? Answer: His lips are moving.

Frank had fed her lies, said he loved her, and now he was in New York, standing at an altar and saying "I do" to another woman.

Enough, Carin thought, and in the middle of the *senhor*'s next joke, she took his hand, pumped it up and down and said it had been a pleasure, an absolute pleasure. Then she let go of his hand, tried not to let the wounded look in his puppy-dog eyes get to her, and made her way out of the living room, through the massive hall and into the library where a string quartet sawed away in direct opposition to the country fiddler holding court in the dining room.

A white-jacketed waiter was threading his way through the crowd, a tray of glasses balanced on his gloved hand.

"Hey," she said to the waiter's back.

It was an inelegant way to draw his attention; she knew her mother would have lifted her eyebrows and told her so, but it worked. The waiter turned towards her and Carin plucked a glass from the tray. This glass was short and squat, filled halfway with an amber liquid and chunks of fruit. She lifted it to her nose, took a sniff, then a sip. "Yuck," she said, but she swallowed another mouthful, anyway.

Amanda came floating by in her husband's arms. "Careful," she sang softly, "or you'll get blot-to."

"Thank you for the sisterly advice," Carin said as her sister sailed off.

Amanda was right. She would get blotto, if she weren't careful. The only one of the three Brewster sisters who could hold liquor was Sam, and Sam wasn't here. She was in Ireland, or France, or England. Wherever, whatever, Sam was probably having fun.

Well, she'd be careful. She didn't want to get drunk. This was, after all, a social event. Not for her, maybe, but for everybody else. For Caitlin, certainly, and for her husband, Tyler Kincaid. She didn't want to spoil their party. Her sister's party. Well, not exactly her sister. Catie was her stepsister... Wasn't she?

Carin drained the last of the amber stuff from the glass and plunked the empty on a table.

The falimial—familial—structure of the Barons, the Brewsters, the Kincaids and now the al Rashids, was complicated. She hiccuped, grinned, and made her way through the library on feet that felt encased in foam rubber.

"Better watch yourself, kid," she whispered.

If she couldn't think "familial," much less say it, it might just be time to slow down the drinking...but not yet.

The hell with it. She was thirsty, and she was an adult. She could drink as much as she wanted.

She hiccuped. Loudly. She giggled, clapped a hand to her mouth and said, "'Scuse me," to nobody in particular.

Somebody laughed. Not at her, surely. People laughed at parties, that was all. Most people came to parties to laugh. To have a good time. Not everyone came to try and forget what a complete ass they'd been made to look, and to feel.

What she needed right now was some fresh air. A cool breeze on her flushed cheeks. Carin made for the doors that led outside.

The thing of it was, Frank had claimed he didn't want to get married. Not ever. She'd told him that was fine and it had been, at first, because what was marriage except two people making vows they never intended to keep? Not the man, anyway.

She slid the doors open, stepped out onto the middle level of Espada's waterfall deck, and drew the soft night air deep into her lungs.

As for sex—how could marriage improve something that wasn't so terrific to start with? Sex was sex, that was all, not the light-up-the-sky stuff people made it out to be.

Still, after a few months she'd started to think it might not be so bad, getting married. Companionship, at the end of the long day spent in her Wall Street office. Someone with whom to share the Sunday paper.

As it turned out, she wasn't the only one who'd changed her mind. Frank had, too. Actually, it was pretty funny. He'd decided he wanted to get married, all right. Just not to her.

Carin swallowed hard.

She had to stop thinking about that. About him. About whatever it was she lacked that he'd found in Iris.

What she needed was something to eat. She hadn't touched food in hours, except for that lobster thingy. And there was a marvelous buffet laid out in the house. Clams, oysters, lobster salad; prime ribs, poached salmon and quail.

What was on the menu at Frank's wedding? She made a face. Snake's belly, most likely, to suit the groom.

What was that? A prickle, on the back of her neck again. Uh-oh. He'd followed her, the Brazilian Bozo. She didn't have to look; who else would it be? She wouldn't even give him the satisfaction of turning around. Let *Senhor* Wonderful try his charms on some female who was interested in playing those games.

Frank had been above game-playing. That was what she'd thought, anyway. It was what she'd initially liked about him.

They'd met at a fund-raiser, and what a revelation he'd been! At least half a dozen men had come on to her that night, all of them using the oldest pickup lines in the world, everything from "Excuse me, but haven't we met before?" to "I just had to tell you, you're the most beautiful woman in the room."

Frank had walked straight up to her, offered his hand and his business card and said he'd heard about her from one of his clients.

"He described you as one of the best investment advisors in New York."

Carin had smiled. "Not one," she'd said. "I *am* the best."

That had been the beginning of their relationship. They saw each other often but she had her life and he had his. That was how they'd both wanted it. Separate existences, no dependency—they'd discussed things honestly and pragmatically. No keys exchanged, no toothbrushes left in either apartment, his or hers.

Had he left a toothbrush in Iris's bathroom?

"Hell," Carin said, and planted her fists on the teak railing.

She was thirsty again. Surely, there was a bar out here. Hadn't Jonas said something about a barbecue on the deck? Was that hickory smoke she smelled, wafting up from the first level? If there was a barbecue, there'd surely be a bar.

Carin headed for the steps. They were wide and straight; she'd never had trouble with them before but tonight, for some reason, she had to hang on to the railing to keep from tripping over her own feet.

"A glass of *sauvignon blanc,* please," she told the bartender when she found him.

Actually, her tongue tripped the way her feet had. What she said sounded more like "A grass of so-vee-on brahnk, pease," and she almost giggled but the bartender gave her a funny look so she looked straight back at him, her brows lifted, her gaze steady. "Well?" she said, and waited.

At last, he poured the wine and gave the glass to her but her hand was, for some reason, unsteady. The pale gold liquid slopped over the side. She frowned, licked the wine from her hand, drained what remained and held out her glass.

"Again," she said.

The bartender shook his head. "Sorry, ma'am."

"Red, then, if you're out of the white." She smiled, to make it clear she really wasn't particular. He didn't smile back.

"I really am sorry, ma'am, but I believe you've had enough."

Carin's eyes narrowed. She leaned forward; the simple action made her woozy but why wouldn't it? This was summer in Texas, even if this was hill country, and the night was warm.

"What do you mean, you think I've had enough? This

is a bar, isn't it? You're a bartender. You're here to pour drinks for people, not to be the sobrie—sobree—not be the 'too much to drink' police.''

"I'll be happy to get you some coffee."

He spoke softly but everyone around them had fallen silent and his words seemed to echo on the night air. Carin flushed.

"Are you saying you think I'm drunk?"

"No, ma'am. But—"

"Then, pour me a drink."

"Ma'am." The bartender leaned towards her. "How about that coffee?"

"Do you know who I am?" Carin heard herself say. She winced mentally, but her mouth seemed to have taken on a life of its own. "Do you know—"

"He knows. And if you do not shut that lovely mouth, so will everyone else."

The voice came from just over her shoulder. It was masculine, low-pitched, and lightly accented. The Latin Lover, Carin thought, and turned around.

"I suppose you think this is your big chance," she said, or started to say, but she didn't finish the sentence.

In spite of the accent, this wasn't the man. This was someone she hadn't seen before. Tipsy or not—and hell, yes, okay, she was, maybe, a little bit potted—she'd have remembered him.

He was tall and broad-shouldered, bigger by far than the guy Amanda had tried to set her up with. His hair was the color of midnight, his eyes the color of storm clouds, and his face was saved from being pretty by a square jaw and a mouth that looked as if it could be as sensual as it could be cruel.

Carin caught her breath. Sober, she'd never have admitted the truth, not even to herself. Tipsy, she could.

He was the stuff of dreams, even, once in a very rare while, the stuff of hers. He was gorgeous, the epitome of masculinity...

And what she did, or said, was none of his business.

"Excuse me?" she said, drawing herself up. Big mistake. Standing straight and taking a deep breath made her head feel as if it didn't actually belong to the rest of her.

"I said—"

"I heard what you said." She poked a finger into the center of his ruffled shirt, against the hard chest beneath the soft linen. "Well, let me tell you something, mister. I don't need your vice. Voice. Advice. And I don't need you to censure—center—censor me, either."

He gave her the kind of look that would have made her cringe, if she hadn't been long beyond the cringing stage.

"You are drunk, *senhora*."

"I'm not a *senhora*. I'm not married. No way, no how, no time."

"All women, single or married, are referred to as *senhora* in my country." His hand closed on her elbow. She glared up at him, tried to tug free, but his grasp on her tightened. "And we do not savor the sight of them drunk, making spectacles of themselves."

His voice was low; she knew it was deliberate, so that none of the curious spectators watching the little tableau could hear what he was saying, and she told herself to take a cue from him, keep things quiet, walk away from the bar, but, dammit, she was not going to take orders from anyone tonight, especially not from a man.

"I'm not interested in your country, or what you do and don't like your women to do. Let go of me."

"*Senhora*, listen to me—"

"Let—go," she repeated, and, when he didn't, she narrowed her eyes, lifted her foot and stepped down, hard, on his instep.

It had to hurt. She was wearing black silk pumps with spiked, three-inch heels. In the self-defense course she'd once taken, the instructor had taught his students to put all their weight and energy into that foot stomp.

The stranger didn't so much as flinch. Instead, he reached out, swung Carin into his arms and, amidst laughter and even a smattering of applause, strode across the deck and down the steps, away from the brightly lit house into the darkness of the garden.

"You—you bastard!" Carin shrieked, beating her fists against his shoulders. "Just who in hell do you think you are?"

"I am Raphael Eduardo Alvares," he said coldly. "And you, Senhora Brewster, are the epitome of a spoiled—"

"Rafe?" Carin's eyes snapped open. She stared, blindly, at the light. "Rafe, where are you?"

"We're losing her," a voice said urgently, and then there was only silence.

CHAPTER TWO

Rio de Ouro, Brazil
Saturday, May 4

RAPHAEL EDUARDO ALVARES shot upright in bed, his heart pounding, his naked body soaked with sweat. He had been dreaming, but of what?

The answer came quickly.

He had been dreaming of the woman again, and the one time he'd been with her.

Rafe threw back the blanket and sat up.

Why? She and the night were nothing but a memory, a memory almost nine months old. Still, the dream had been so real, and not the same as it always was. In this dream, she'd been hurt. In an accident, perhaps. And she was calling out to him...

Not that it mattered. The woman meant nothing to him. Besides, he didn't believe in dreams. What a man could see and touch, that was what mattered. Dreams were foolishness, and only led to pain.

Rafe rose to his feet, stretched and walked to the window. Dawn was just touching the sky; the endless savannah stretched under its pale pink glow all the way to the low, dark hills in the distance.

It was good he had awakened early. He was flying to São Paulo this morning for a business meeting, and then for lunch with Claudia. He'd told his pilot to have the plane ready by eight. Now he'd have a couple of hours to do some work first.

By the time Rafe showered, shaved and dressed, the dream was forgotten. He went downstairs, greeted his housekeeper, took the cup of sweet, black coffee she handed him and went down the hall, to his office.

Twenty minutes later, he shut down his computer and gave up. He couldn't concentrate. He was thinking about the dream again. And about the woman. Would he never be able to get her out of his head?

Rafe reached for the phone.

Might as well move up his departure...but once he had his pilot on the line, he canceled the flight entirely. After that, he telephoned São Paulo, left messages of regret on the answering machine of the man he'd intended to meet and then on Claudia's. She never stirred until late morning; he still remembered that. There was no reason to think she'd changed, even in the five years since he'd ended their engagement.

His behavior was out of character, he knew. Not putting aside lunch with Claudia. She'd pout, but it was not a problem. Canceling his meeting—that was different. He had not built his empire of horses, cattle and banks by doing things precipitously, but what was the logic of trying to concentrate on business when his thoughts were not in Brazil but tangled in a dream that made no sense?

Even if Carin were in trouble, he was the last man in the world she would want beside her.

Rafe changed into a black T-shirt, faded jeans and the scuffed riding boots he'd owned since he'd come to Rio de Ouro more than a decade before. Perhaps a long ride would clear his head. Down at the stables, he waved off his men, led his horse from its stall and saddled it. He mounted the stallion and touched its flanks lightly with his heels.

He'd put the Brewster woman out of his thoughts months ago, and with good reason. She'd made it clear that what had happened meant nothing. An hour was all she'd wanted of him...one hour, when he'd stood in for another man.

Not that he'd wanted more of her. He'd only sought her out in the first place because courtesy demanded it. He'd been a guest at a party he'd had no real wish to attend, and one of his hostess's daughters—the wife of a friend, in fact, the very friend who'd introduced him to Jonas Baron, and to the Baron stables—had said that she hoped he'd meet her sister.

The rest of the Barons had hinted at the same thing.

"Gonna be lots a' good-lookin' women at the party," Jonas had told him, and grinned. "Sounds like a pretty fine weekend to me, Alvares. Spend the day vettin' that stallion you're interested in, spend the evenin' checkin' out some of Texas's finest fillies."

Marta Baron had smiled as Jonas handed her a sherry. "My husband is right, you know. There'll be some charming young women at the party. I'm sure they'll all want to meet you."

"How nice," Rafe had replied, lying politely. Why did women of a certain age seem to view all unmarried males as a challenge? "But I hadn't planned on staying for the party—"

"Oh, please do!" Amanda al Rashid took her husband's arm. "Really, Rafe, it'll be fun. My sister, Carin, will be flying in from New York. Did I mention that?"

Warning bells rang in Rafe's head. He knew that smile, knew that all-too-casual tone of voice.

"No," he'd said, even more politely, "you didn't."

"Ah. Well, she is. And I just know you'll hit it off."

"I'm sure we will," Rafe had replied.

That had been lie number two. He had no such expectation but then, he'd been down this road before. Many times, in fact. Mothers, aunts, the wives of his business acquaintances…there were moments he could almost believe that every woman on the planet had a daughter, sister or niece she was certain he'd like.

It went, as the North Americans said, with the territory. He was thirty-four, he was single; he had money and property and, according to the things women said to him in bed, he supposed he had what were known as good looks. The only thing he didn't have was a wife—but why would he want one?

Still, he hadn't wished to insult his host, his hostess, his friend and his friend's wife, all at the same time. So he'd stayed for the party and gone looking for the woman. A polite hello, followed by an equally polite apology for retiring early, had seemed simple enough.

Except, it hadn't worked out that way.

Rafe reined in the horse and stared blindly into the distance. Instead of finding the woman, he'd found a spitting, hissing, wildcat.

And he'd taken her to bed.

He'd had many women in his life. More than his share, some would say, but never one like her.

The way she had gone into his arms, as if he were the only man she'd ever wanted. The wildness in her kisses. The way her body had hummed with delight under his hands and mouth. *Deus,* she'd set him on fire. Her climax had made him feel as omnipotent as a god; his, seconds later, had shaken him to the depths of his soul. But when he'd tried to draw her close, she'd pushed free of his embrace, asked him to leave in a way that made it clear he'd served his purposes and was being dismissed.

She had gone into the bathroom. He'd heard the click of the lock and for one insane moment, he'd thought of kicking down the door, carrying her back to bed and showing her that she could not use a man and then discard him as if he were trash...

Rafe's mouth thinned.

The boy he'd once been might have done such a thing. The man he'd become would not. Instead, he'd dressed in the dark, gone to his room in the silent, sleeping house...

The horse snorted and danced beneath him. Rafe patted the proudly arched neck. Carin Brewster was not simply a distant memory, she was an unpleasant one.

Then, why couldn't he get her out of his head?

His vision blurred as he remembered that night, how someone had laughed and pointed to Carin, when he'd asked where she was; how he'd stood on the deck of a Texas mansion, watching her make a fool of herself while people smirked, and wondered if he ought to be a gentleman and do something about it or just let the scene play out...

Hell. He wasn't a gentleman. He never would be.

But Jonas Baron was his host and Nick al Rashid was his friend, which made Nick's wife his friend, too, and the woman making a fool of herself was Amanda al Rashid's sister...

Without any more thought than that, Rafe strode towards Carin, scooped her into his arms and carried her down the steps and towards the garden. People saw it happen; they laughed and cheered but nobody tried to stop him—nobody except the wildcat in his arms, who was kicking and cursing and beating at his shoulders with her fists.

That Nick's wife and her mother would even imagine he'd be interested in the kicking, cursing woman he was carrying deep into the garden, seemed impossible.

Carin Brewster was the very antithesis of the sort of woman he'd someday search out and marry because, yes, he supposed he would marry, eventually. A man needed heirs so that all he'd sweated and struggled to build would not be lost, but the woman he'd choose to be his wife would be compliant and faithful. She would want to devote herself to him and to the children she would bear him.

That was the whole reason for marriage, wasn't it?

"Are you crazy?" Carin shrieked, as he carried her further from the house. "Put me down!"

No wonder the woman's family was having such difficulty marrying her off. She was beautiful, yes. She was also sharp-tongued, evil-tempered and self-centered. Rafe could hardly wait to get rid of her.

"You idiot!" She pounded her fists against his chest. "You—you moron! Do you have any idea who I am?"

"Yes," Rafe said coldly, "I know precisely who you are."

"You can't just grab a woman and carry her off like this!"

"Ah," he said calmly, jerking his head back just in time to avoid a wildly thrown punch, "if only you'd mentioned that sooner, *senhora*. I wouldn't have done it."

"You—you—you…"

She called him a name that implied he was related to the scatological habits of canines. He laughed. That only made her more furious. She flailed out with her fists again; this time, her knuckles dusted his jaw.

Deus.

There was a saying in this country about being careful not to catch a tiger by the tail without having a plan for letting it go.

What *was* he going to do with Carin Brewster?

"You just wait! Oh, you just wait until I get back to the house. I'll have you thrown off this property so fast it'll make your head spin."

"I am—how do you say? I am shaking in my boots."

"Quaking. And you'd damn well better be." Carin pounded his chest again. "For the last time, put me down!"

"If I do, will you go to your room, ask the housekeeper to bring you a pot of black coffee and drink every drop?"

"Why should I?"

"Because you are drunk."

"I am no such thing."

"You are drunk," Rafe said firmly, "and you were making a spectacle of yourself."

"If you were correct...*if* you were correct, it would be my business, not yours. You had no right to interfere."

"I interfered on behalf of your family, and on behalf of the poor young man you were threatening."

"That's pathetic. Do you really expect me to believe that?"

"Actually, I did it for your sister, who thinks a great deal of you."

"You don't know a thing about what my sister thinks."

"On the contrary, *senhora*. I know that she has false illusions about you, or she would not have assumed I might find you appealing."

"Yeah, well, she has the same illusions about you, you—you South American Neanderthal. And if you're really thinking about my family, start concentrating on how they'll react when I tell them what you did."

"Nicholas and Jonas would surely agree a gag might be an excellent idea." Rafe shifted her weight in his arms. She was slender and fine-boned but she wriggled and twisted like a snake. Holding on to her and ducking those flying fists wasn't easy. He thought of tossing her over his shoulder, thought of all the alcohol he'd seen her consume, and decided against it. "As for your stepbrothers..." He looked down at her, his expression severe. "I have met them. And from what I know of Tyler, Gage, Travis and Slade, they would..."

Rafe came to a halt. There was a clearing just ahead. Teak benches ringed a subtly lighted reflecting pool into which a stone nymph emptied an endless stream of water from a copper ewer.

"They would what?" the warm, sweet-smelling, bad-tempered burden in his arms demanded.

"They would applaud me for what I am about to do."

With that, he marched up to the pool and dumped her straight into it.

She landed on her bottom, legs splayed, up to her hips in water. Showered and sober, he thought with satisfaction, because the nymph was no longer emptying the ewer into the pool, she was emptying it over Carin Brewster's head.

A hush fell over everything. Even the cascading water seemed to grow silent. Carin's mouth opened; her lips formed a stunned, "Oh..."

And then she let out a blood-curdling shriek.

What a pity, to ruin such a lovely dress, Rafe thought dispassionately. What there was of it. Black silk, cut low enough to show the ripe curves of her breasts, high enough to show the long length of her legs. Wet, the silk clung lovingly to her body; he saw her nipples peak from the sudden chill of the water.

Beautiful, indeed, but that was all. She was nothing a man in his right mind would want...

Not for a lifetime, no. But she might prove interesting, for a night.

With heart-stopping swiftness, Rafe felt his body respond. It would be a challenge, getting past that hot temper, searching out ways to turn the fury in those dark eyes to passion. He could do it, though. He could tame her in bed, as he had tamed her here.

He imagined stripping off that black dress and the hint of black lace he could see beneath it, letting those long legs close around him as he cupped that lovely face in his hands and tasted that full, soft-looking mouth...

Deus. Was he crazy? Carin Brewster was beautiful but the Baron mansion was, as Jonas had promised, filled with beautiful women who were sweet-tempered, soft-spoken and sober, though he suspected Carin was sober enough, now. The combination of anger, adrenaline and cold water would have ended her alcoholic haze.

Yes, he thought, as he looked down at her, it had. Her shrieks had turned into moans; she was holding her hands to her temples as she tried to struggle to her feet.

Despite himself, he felt a stab of pity. He hesitated, then moved closer, bent down and held out his hand.

"Here," he said, "take my hand."

The woman looked at it as if it were a snake with its fangs bared. He supposed he could hardly blame her.

"Do you hear me, *senhora?* Take my hand and I'll help you up."

"I'd sooner stay here all night."

"Are you determined to go on behaving like a spoiled brat? Let me help you."

"I'm perfectly capable of helping myself."

She tried to prove it by scrambling to her feet but she slipped on the wet marble, made a wild grab at the air, and Rafe ended up with her in his arms again.

"Do not do that," she said furiously. "Just put me—"

"—down," he said. "Yes, most assuredly, that is what I intend to do." He set her on her feet, peeled off his jacket and draped it around her shoulders. She tried to shrug it off but he lifted her hair free of the collar—the water had ruined the curls that had been swept up high on her head. He drew the lapels together and held the jacket closed.

"I don't need your jacket. I don't need anything from you."

"You are cold."

"I am wet," Carin snapped, "and if you try very, very hard, you might just be able to figure out the reason."

"You were drunk."

"And?"

"And, now you are not."

"Wonderful. Is that some special Brazilian method used to deal with hangovers? Didn't you ever hear of black coffee?"

"I suggested coffee, but you declined it."

"And so you d-d-decided to take th-things into your own hands."

He frowned. "Your teeth are chattering."

"So wou-would yours, if s-someone dropped you in a f-fountain."

"Come." He reached for her; she drew back.

"I'm n-not going anyplace w-with you."

She lifted her chin and glared at him. Rafe thought about arguing, thought better of it, sighed and hoisted her into his arms again.

"Hey!" Her voice rose as he started back through the gardens. "Do you have a d-death w-wish? I told you, my family w-will…"

"They will visit you in the hospital," he said grimly, "if you don't behave yourself and get out of those wet clothes and into a hot shower."

"That I'm soaked to the skin isn't your pr-problem, dammit, it's your f-fault!"

"You're also sober, or haven't you considered that?"

"I can't be sober. I mean, assuming I were drunk, which I wasn't, how could I be sober five minutes later?"

"Cold water. There are times, if one is fortunate, it has that effect."

"How would you know?"

"A man knows these things." Especially if he'd ever had one drink too many, trying to prove himself in a backwater bar on the Amazon, Rafe thought, and shuddered. "Put your arms around my neck, please, Senhora Brewster."

"I'll do no such thing."

Rafe sighed, debated the wisdom of tossing her over his shoulder and, once again, decided against it.

"Is there an entrance to the house that will permit us to avoid the other guests? Unless, of course, you prefer a dramatic entrance. It might be quite effective, considering the exit you made."

"That's your story, *senhor,* but you were the one who made the scene."

"The bartender might not agree."

"What bar..." she began to say, and then he heard her catch her breath. He knew it was all coming back to her and that once it had, she would be crushed. "Oh. That bartender." She cleared her throat. "I—I remember now."

"Indeed?"

"Yes. At least, I remember some of... Tell me the truth. Did I—was I—" She cleared her throat again. "I made an ass of myself, didn't I?"

Rafe hesitated. She had, but what was the point in telling her that? "You were—how do you say it—you were a bit high-spirited."

"In other words," she said in a small voice, "the answer is 'yes.'"

"People forget," he said briskly.

"They're not likely to forget a woman who has to be carried off like a—a bad joke."

Rafe decided to take pity on her. "What they will remember," he said, "is that a man was so taken with your beauty that he could not bear sharing you with others."

"That's very generous. If I didn't know the truth, I might almost believe you."

"It is the story I will tell tomorrow, if I am asked."

"That's more than generous, *senhor,* it's gallant. And yes, there's a back door. It's just past those shrubs."

The door opened at a touch. It led into an enormous pantry, which was empty.

"You can put me down," Carin said.

Rafe thought about it. He could. But, he reminded himself, it was his fault she was wet and cold. How could he abandon her now?

"I will see you to your room, *senhora.* Just tell me where it is."

She told him, and he made his way quickly to the service stairs and to the second floor.

"That door," she said, "the one on the left."

Carin reached out and opened the door; Rafe elbowed it closed behind them. Her bedroom smelled faintly of her perfume.

"You can put me down now."

He nodded. "Of course," he replied...but he didn't. He didn't. He stood in the darkness, holding her in his arms, wondering how she could smell like jasmine and roses after being dropped in a pool of water and wondering, too, why his arms were tightening around her even as he told himself to put her on her feet.

"*Senhor.*" She drew a breath, then let it out. It stroked his skin like silk. "I—I think I owe you an apology."

"I accept." He smiled. "But only if you call me Rafe."

Carin laughed. "You were supposed to say that an apology wasn't necessary."

"But it is. You called me many names tonight and, truly, I only deserved some of them."

She laughed again, leaned back in the curve of his arm and looked into his face.

"All right. I'm sorry. Honestly, I am."

Deus, she was lovely. And charming, now that she was sober. But she needed to undress, and to get warm and dry. He could help her with all of that, he thought, and felt his body quicken again.

Carefully, he set her on her feet. "You must get out of your wet clothing, Carin, and take a hot shower."

"I know." She hesitated. "Rafe? I—I wouldn't want you to think...I mean, really, it was good of you to come to my rescue, but—" She pushed a strand of hair behind her ear. "I just want you to know that I don't usually drink like that."

He nodded. He'd already come to that conclusion. "I am certain that is the case."

"In fact, I've never done anything like it before. It's just that—that..." She fell silent. She owed this stranger no explanation yet, somehow, she wanted to offer one, but what could she say that wouldn't make her look even more pathetic? "Never mind." She smiled, held out her hand. "Thank you for everything."

He nodded, took her hand in his. She'd been on the verge of telling him what had happened that had made her want to forget. That was, after all, why people drank. To forget. To heal pain and yes, despite her smile, he could see pain in her eyes. Who had hurt her? A man? If that were true, he deserved to be beaten. This woman was too fragile, too beautiful...

Rafe drew away his hand and stepped back.

"I am glad I was there to be of service," he said politely.

"And now, you must get warm. Shall I ask one of the servants to bring you some hot soup?"

"No. No, I'll be fine." She slipped his jacket off her shoulders. "Do you want to take your jacket, or shall I wait and have it pressed…"

Her words dwindled to silence. He knew the reason; his gaze had dropped to her breasts and her nipples had beaded instantly, to thrust against the damp silk.

"Carin." Her eyes met his. There was something else there now, not pain, not despair. Indeed, what he saw made his blood throb. He reached out; she stepped back but he clasped her wrists and stopped her. "Why did you do it?" His tone was rough, almost urgent. "Why did you do that to yourself tonight?"

"This was—it was a difficult weekend for me." She licked her lips. "That's really why I came to the party. I wasn't going to, but my sister thought it would be a good idea. Obviously, she was wrong."

Rafe smiled. "An interesting woman, your sister."

"What do you mean?"

"She urged me to meet you. She said you were beautiful, and charming, and that I would find you fascinating."

Carin blushed. "She didn't!"

"No." He grinned. "Not exactly, but she certainly made it clear that she thought you and I would be a good match."

"Oh, isn't that awful?" Carin rolled her eyes. "Actually, she talked you up, too. She said you were this incredibly handsome, incredibly charming, incredibly everything man. I just had to meet you, she said, because you were—"

"Incredible," Rafe said, and they both laughed.

"Uh-huh. And I figured, if Mandy thought you such a paragon—"

"—you wanted no part of me." He was still holding her wrists. Now, he lifted them and brushed his lips across the backs of her hands. "Nor I, of you. It was, how do you say, too much of a buildup."

"I'm sure she never mentioned I'd be doing my best to get pie-eyed."

"Pie...? Ah." He grinned. "No. No, she did not." Slowly, his smile faded. "Are you going to tell me what this thing was, that happened to you? That made you want to drink yourself into oblivion tonight?"

He watched the swift play of emotions in her face, knew she was considering a dozen different easy answers, and saw the instant when she decided to tell him the truth.

"A man who once meant something to me is..." She hesitated. "He's getting married tonight."

"Ah." Another strand of dark hair slipped across her cheek. Rafe stroked it away from her face again but this time, he let his hand linger against her skin. She was so soft to the touch. So beautiful. What sort of man would want another woman, when he could have her?

"I am sorry you were hurt, *querida.*"

"Don't be. Besides, that's no excuse. I shouldn't have behaved like a fool."

His hands cupped her face. He tilted it up to his, his thumbs stroking across her cheekbones.

"It is this man you mourn who is the fool, not you."

"Thank you. It's kind of you to try and make me feel better, but really—"

"Do you think I would tell you such a thing if I didn't believe it?" He clasped her shoulders and drew her towards him. "What man would want another woman, if he could have you?"

He bent his head and kissed her, gently at first, the merest brush of his mouth on hers. He told himself he meant this kiss as reassurance but she looked up at him, her lips parted, the pulse pounding, hard, in the hollow of her throat, and he knew he'd been lying to himself.

He'd kissed her because he wanted her taste on his tongue.

"Carin." He cupped her face in his hands and kissed her again, more deliberately, and just when he thought he'd misread what he'd seen in her eyes, she moaned and brought her body against his, opened her mouth and kissed him back.

He could feel his heart thundering. He wanted her, wanted her as he could not recall ever wanting a woman before. Some still-logical part of his brain warned him that wanting her so desperately made no sense, that taking her when she was longing for another man could only be an error, but now she was digging her hands into his hair, bringing his head down to hers, seeking his tongue with her own.

Rafe stopped thinking.

He groaned and gathered her close, ran his hand down her back, lifted her into him, tilting her so that she could feel his hardness straining against her. When she moaned and moved against him, he drew back, even though it took every bit of self-control he possessed.

"Look at me, Carin," he said roughly. "Look at me, and see that I am not the man who lost you."

"I know that." She put her hands flat against his chest. "But you are the man I want."

Rafe swept her into his arms, carried her to the bed. She was like flame, burning with need. She was silk under his hands, under his mouth…

"Senhor Raphael!"

The cry brought him back to reality. He blinked, tore his thoughts from that night and saw his houseman galloping towards him on the back of a lathered mare. His gut clenched. João feared horses; the men teased him mercilessly. He never rode, they said, unless disaster was imminent.

Rafe tugged on the reins, rode to meet him. "What is it?"

"A telephone call, *senhor,* from a woman who gives her name as Amanda Brewster al Rashid. She says it is urgent, that it concerns her sister..."

"Carin," Rafe whispered.

He spurred his horse, bent low over the outstretched neck, and raced for the house.

CHAPTER THREE

RAFE. Rafe, where are you?

Carin cried out in silence, her voice echoing only inside her head.

This is a dream, she kept telling herself, only a dream. Open your eyes and wake up.

She couldn't. Her lids felt as if they'd been weighted with lead, her lashes glued to her cheeks. The more she tried, the tighter the dream held her. Still, she fought to leave it. The rational part of her mind warned her that if she were to succumb to the dark, the path she took would lead to nothingness.

Eventually, the darkness began loosening its hold. She floated in a kind of foggy twilight. Voices penetrated the silence, urging her to open her eyes and leave the dream behind.

Wake up, Carin.

Come on, Ms. Brewster. Open your eyes.

Carin, sweetie, please, please, look at me.

She recognized the voices. Her doctor. Her sister. She heard her mother and her stepfather, too, but what were they all doing here? What? she asked herself desperately, and felt herself floating away…but the voices wouldn't let it happen.

"Carin," her doctor said, "come on, Carin. It's time to wake up."

"Oh, darling," Marta said, "look at us, please. Can you do that, Carin?"

"Carrie," Amanda said firmly, "stop this nonsense and open your eyes right now."

She almost smiled, then. Nobody had called her "Carrie" in years and years.

And then a hand took hers. Warm, strong fingers pressed into her own, entwined with hers.

"Carin," a voice whispered, close to her ear. "Do you hear me? You must open your eyes now and look at me."

Rafe? Was he here, holding her hand, sitting beside her and offering her comfort as he had done once before? Of course not. She had been dreaming of him again, just as she had during the past months, and wasn't that dumb because he'd made it clear he never wanted to see her again.

Not that she wanted to see him. What they'd done—what she'd done—was wrong. Ugly. Shameful. Never mind the excitement of it, the heat of his hands, the ecstasy of feeling him deep inside her...

"Rafe," Carin whispered, "Rafe?" and she came awake in a dizzying rush to find herself, alone, in a world of cold reality and confused memories.

That night. Oh, God, that terrible night. Making love with Rafe—except, it hadn't been love. It had been sex, sex with a stranger. He'd give her what she'd wanted, passion that had driven everything else from her mind, but when it was over she'd been filled with such self-loathing that she'd struggled free of his arms, gone into the bathroom, locked the door and leaned back against it, trembling, afraid he'd come after her...

Praying that he would.

She needn't have worried.

No one had knocked at the bathroom door. No one rattled the knob. No one said, "Carin, come back to my arms." When she'd finally come out of the bathroom, Rafe was gone. He wasn't downstairs, either. There'd been no message. No note. No phone call waiting on her answering machine in New York or in all the months that came after.

One hour. One unbelievable, wondrous, terrible hour, was all it had been...

Except, that wasn't true. Carin's heartbeat lurched. Raphael Alvares had given her more than that night.

He'd given her a child.

The long hours of labor. Amanda, holding her hand. The doctor's decision to hasten her baby's entry into the world...

"My baby," she said, the words a tremulous, desperate whisper.

She touched her hand to her belly. It was flat. Her baby had been born—her daughter, she'd known that in advance—but where was she? Something had gone wrong, at the end. She remembered, now. Her doctor, telling her to hang on. The slap-slap of a nurse's shoes as she hurried from the room. The plastic packet of blood hanging above her, dripping into her vein...

Carin shot up against the pillows. Her head spun, her stomach seesawed in protest.

"Where's my baby?"

"Carin?"

She turned her head, saw bright light streaming into the room as the door opened. Shapes—people—were silhouetted against it.

"Carin," her mother said, "oh, sweetie!"

And then Marta's arms were around her. Carin wept and clung to her as the others crowded around. Jonas was there, and Amanda, even her stepbrother, Slade, and his wife, Lara...

But not Rafe. Of course not. He'd only been a dream.

Hands patted her shoulders, touched her hair. Her mother's light scent enveloped her; she felt her sister's tears as their cheeks brushed.

"That's my girl," Marta said, and made a sound that straddled the line between laughter and tears. "Oh, darling, it's so good to see you awake. How do you feel? Are you in pain? Lara, please, would you go get the nurse?"

"Of course," Lara Baron said, and blew a kiss before hurrying off.

"Tell me about my baby," Carin begged. "Mandy? Is she all right?"

"She's fine." Amanda sat down on the edge of the bed and clasped her hand. "And she's beautiful."

Carin fell back against the pillows. Tears rose in her eyes and she laughed and rubbed them away with her knuckles.

"I want to know everything. Is she big? What color is her hair? What does she weigh?"

"She's seven pounds, five ounces and twenty-one inches long, and she has a head full of midnight-black curls. Oh, Sis, she's perfect."

Carin squeezed her sister's hand. "I want to see her."

"And you will, darling." Marta embraced Carin again. "In just a little while, I promise. Let's have the doctor take a look at you first, hmm?"

"I don't need the doctor."

"You're probably right, but it won't hurt to let him see you, will it?" Marta pulled a lace-trimmed hankie from her purse and dabbed at her eyes. "He said—he said he was sure the crisis was over and you'd be fine, but we were all—we were…"

Her voice broke. Jonas put his hand on his wife's shoulder, patted it clumsily and smiled at Carin.

"You sure did give us a bad time for a while there, missy."

"Did I?" She shook her head. "I don't—I don't remember very much."

"No. I don't suppose you would. Never mind. All that matters is that everything's fine, now."

"Where is my baby? Is she in the nursery?"

"Uh-huh." Amanda grinned. "And she's making all the other little girls look homely by comparison."

"Amanda's right." Marta smiled as she stroked Carin's hair back from her temples. "She looks just like you, darling. Well, except for her mouth. I suppose she has her father's…'' Everyone looked at Marta, who colored. ''I mean, she's gorgeous.''

Carin sighed. ''I'll bet she is.'' She looked past her mother, at Slade, and smiled. ''What are you doing here?''

''Well, Lara and I had nothin' better to do…'' He grinned. ''Boston's only a hop, skip, and jump away, honey. We figured we'd come down and wait for you to open your eyes.''

''That was sweet of you.''

''Heck, the Barons are nothin' if not sweet.'' He walked to the other side of the bed and took her hand. ''Travis, Tyler and Gage all send their love.''

''Give mine to them, please, when you talk to them.''

''And,'' Amanda said, ''my Nicholas will be by, in a little while.'' Tears rose in her eyes and she brushed them away. ''You gave us a real scare, Sis.''

''Well, I didn't mean to,'' Carin said, and smiled. She let her head fall back against the pillows and her smile faded. ''I'm sorry I put you through all of this.''

''There's nothing to be sorry about,'' Marta said. ''I just wish you'd come to stay with us at Espada, months ago…'' She cleared her throat. ''Well, that's all water under the bridge. The important thing is that you've come through this, and that you have a healthy baby.''

Carin nodded. ''I just wish…'' She swallowed past the sudden lump in her throat. ''I wish it could have been different. That—that I hadn't disappointed all of you.''

''Nonsense, darling. Who could be disappointed at having a new little person in our family?''

''I told her the same thing, Mother.'' Amanda looked up as Lara came into the room. ''Doctor's coming,'' she mouthed, and Amanda nodded. ''I said we'd all be in this with her, that she didn't have to face it by herself.''

''Damn right,'' Slade growled. ''Whatever happened to the idea of Responsibility, with a capital *R*?'' Lara shot him a warning look and he frowned. "Well, hell, it's the truth, Sugar, isn't it? If Carin had told us, right off, one of us Barons—hell, all of us—would have gone down there to Brazil and—"

"Brazil?" Carin struggled up against the pillows. "What do you mean, you'd have gone to Brazil?" Her eyes flashed to her sister. "I never told you about—about anything."

Amanda cleared her throat. "Uh, no. No, you didn't. Not—not at first."

"Not at first? Not ever. You asked and asked and asked, but I never said—"

"Actually, you did." Amanda hesitated. "Look, why don't we discuss this another time? When you're feeling stronger."

"I feel strong enough now. What do you mean, 'actually' I did?"

"You were groggy, Sis. And you—you called for him. For Raphael Alvares."

Carin turned pale. "And you told everyone else? Oh, Mandy, why? Why did you do that?"

"I didn't tell anyone. Well, only Nick, but—"

"Then, how does Slade know?"

"He just—he just knows," Amanda said, and shot Slade a look.

"He knows, because you told him. And what for? I certainly don't want any of you hustling off to Brazil to tell Rafe that he—he fathered my child."

"Well," Jonas said, "fact is, nobody has to do that, 'cause—"

"The fact is that no one will," Marta said. Jonas snorted, and she cleared her throat. "Go to Brazil, I mean."

"I hope not. Raphael Alvares is the last man I want to see."

"Sweetie," Marta said gently, "you don't mean that."

"I mean every word."

"Maybe now's not the best time to make decisions,"

Jonas said. "You might want to think about things. And your baby's got a stake in this, missy." He ran a finger around the inside of his shirt collar. "Maybe I learned it a little late but a kid's got the right to grow up knowin' who his...who her father is."

"Look," Carin said wearily, "I know you all mean well, that you want to protect me and my daughter, but you have to understand, I did the right thing. Things were different for you and Tyler, Jonas—"

"Things are always different," Slade said gruffly. "But a man's entitled to know he's a father, and to tell you how he feels about it. A woman denies him that right, he might do anything to claim his—"

"Slade, for heaven's sakes!" Marta glared at her stepson. "Must we discuss this now?"

"You're right." He took a deep breath. "Carin, honey, I'm sorry."

"No, it's okay. I know you're worried about me but trust me, this is—it's different than it was for you, Jonas, or for you, Slade..."

"Yeah, sure." Slade hesitated, then bent down and pressed his lips to Carin's forehead. "Just keep something in mind," he said softly. "Men aren't always the enemy, kid."

"I know." She smiled, took his hand and brought it to her cheek. "I can think of a few who might even qualify as good guys."

But not Raphael Alvares. She couldn't imagine anyone thinking of him as a good guy. Still, he was the kind of man Slade had described, one who'd do whatever it took to get what he wanted. As little as she knew about Rafe, she was certain he'd move heaven and earth to claim a thing, if he wanted it badly enough.

He hadn't wanted her.

She made a soft sound of distress. Marta grabbed her hand.

"Carin? Darling, what is it?"

"Nothing. Really, I'm fine." She smiled and pressed her mother's hand in reassurance. "I'm—I'm a little achy, that's all."

"Well, of course you are. Achy, and all worn out, and here we are, giving you lectures when we should be letting you rest." Marta kissed her, then turned towards the others. "I have an idea," she said briskly. "Slade, you go find us some coffee. Jonas, you wait in the lounge. Lara, you and I will go hunt down that doctor…"

Carin grabbed for Amanda's hand as the Barons filed from the room. "Mandy?"

Amanda leaned towards her. "Mmm?"

"I want you to promise me you won't do anything."

"Anything about what?"

"You know what. I don't want you getting the same silly idea everybody else seems to have about getting in touch with—with Rafe."

Amanda colored. "Well—well, actually, Sis, when you kept calling his name, I thought—I mean, you seemed to want…"

"Not him," Carin said fiercely. "Never him!"

"Well—well don't worry about any of that now, okay? Just concentrate on getting better." Amanda's voice softened. "And think about that little girl of yours, about how you'll want to do all the right things for her."

"Oh, I will." Carin sighed. "I can't wait to see her."

"Look, why don't I see if I can get the nurse to bring the baby to you right now?"

"Would you?"

"Sure." Amanda put her arms around Carin and hugged her. "Meanwhile, just shut your eyes and rest, okay, Sis?"

"Okay," Carin said, and yawned.

The door swung softly closed. Carin yawned again, closed her eyes and let her thoughts drift. Her baby. Her very own little girl. She could hardly wait to see her. Would she look like her father?

Rafe was so handsome. Those deep, dark eyes. That dark, silky hair. The firm mouth, that had felt so wonderful against hers...

He'd been such an incredible lover.

Strong. Powerful. His body hard and hot as he'd moved above her. His hands, all-knowing and clever, touching her in ways Frank had never touched her, until she'd cried out, arched against him, and then he'd slipped his hands beneath her, lifted her to him, entered her slowly, slowly, buried himself inside her.

She'd come even as he entered her, come again and again, and that had never happened to her before. She'd never flown so fast, so high, never wanted the night to last forever, the arms that held her to hold her forever...

Her eyes flew open. What was she thinking?

She'd just given birth. Sex was the last thing she ought to have on her mind and besides, why did she keep romanticizing what had happened? Rafe hadn't even tried to pretend that taking her to bed had meant something; he'd walked away from her as if she were the cheap slut she'd made herself out to be.

Her throat constricted.

What did any of that matter now? She was tired, that was all. Overwrought, by what she'd just gone through. Rafe didn't mean a thing to her; he never had. What she'd wanted from him was what he'd given her, oblivion in his arms, and if memories of that night still haunted her, it only proved how truly pathetic she was.

"Carin?"

Carin opened her eyes. The room was empty, except for her doctor, who stood beside the bed.

"Doctor." She sat up, her eyes bright with anticipation. "I want to see my daughter."

"Yes," he said, and grinned, "so they tell me. Just give

me five minutes to check you over, and I'll tell them to bring her to you.''

"Five minutes," Carin said, and smiled back at him, "not a second more."

"You have my word. Okay, let's take a look. Lie back a little... That's the girl. You're coming along just fine, Carin. Take a deep breath. Let it out slowly. Good. I'm sure you know that when you leave here, you'll need time to recover."

"I'll take a couple of weeks off."

"Well, you'll want more than a couple of weeks. You'll be tired, for a while. You'll need somebody to relieve you with the baby, give you the chance to rest."

"I'm strong as an ox, Doctor. I'll be on my feet in no time."

"Yeah, you will, but if you push things, you're liable to regret it. And you won't want to have that happen, for the baby's sake. Now, let's just check that belly..."

"I'll work something out," she said, as the doctor gently poked and prodded. "Tell me about my baby. My sister says she's fine. Is she?"

"Better than fine. Got the best pair of lungs in the nursery, all the requisite fingers and toes. A regular little beauty. Does it hurt when I press here?"

"No." Carin winced. "Well, just a little."

"That's okay. You're doing great." The doctor straightened up and smiled at her as he tucked his stethoscope back into his pocket. "Remember how panicked you were when you first came to see me, and how I said everything would work out? And it has. You've learned that your family is thrilled about your baby, and that her father wants to be part of her life and yours. I think that's all pretty remarkable."

"Yes, I suppose it..." Carin froze. "What?"

"I said, I think it's remark—"

"You must be confusing me with another patient. My

baby's father didn't know about my pregnancy. He doesn't know about my daughter. And he never will."

The doctor cleared his throat. "Well, of course, that's all up to you. Meanwhile, suppose I tell the nurse to arrange for a visit with your little girl?"

"That would be wonderful."

"Fine." The doctor took her hand. "One last thing…"

"Yes?"

"Things change, Carin. It's possible to be sure you're on the right path in life and then, all of a sudden, you discover you were meant to take another."

"I've already learned that," she said softly.

"Yes, well, sometimes we learn the same lesson in more than one—ah." He swung towards the door as it opened. "Here's your baby now."

Carin sat up. The doctor patted her shoulder again, then made his way to the door. His bulky figure blocked her view and she shifted on the bed, trying for her first glimpse of her child.

"My little girl," she said softly.

"And mine," a voice said coldly. "At least, that's the story I've been told."

Her eyes flew from her daughter to the face of the man holding the child in his arms.

It was Raphael Alvares.

CHAPTER FOUR

HE WAS here.

The dream had been real. Rafe had come for her...

But he hadn't. Another look at his face, and Carin knew that. He wasn't here for her. She couldn't think of a reason he would be...unless one of her stepbrothers had done something incredibly stupid.

"Querida," he said.

The tone of his voice, the little half smile on his lips, turned the endearment into a mockery.

"Rafe." She cleared her throat. Fear danced along her spine but that was silly. What was there to be afraid of? Slade, or another of the Barons, had sent for him. All she had to do was tell him they'd been wrong to do that...

"You seem surprised to see me, Carin."

"Yes. I—I am. What—what are you doing here?"

He gave her a twisted smile and walked towards the bed. "Why, *querida,* I am here to see you, of course." He glanced at the sleeping infant in his arms. "And to see your daughter."

Carin's gaze flew to the baby, then to him. "What are you doing with my baby?"

"Don't you mean, what am I doing with *our* baby? That seems to be the consensus, *querida,* that this child is mine." His lips curved in another tight smile. "One of the nurses thought a father should become acquainted with his offspring. I decided to indulge her in her little fantasy."

Carin's color heightened. "Give me my daughter."

"Certainly," he said politely. "But first, perhaps, you'd be good enough to tell me why you've claimed I am her father?"

"I don't know what you're talking about." Her voice sharpened. "Give her to me, Rafe."

He did as she'd asked. She cradled the tiny bundle against her breasts, crooned to the child and pressed a kiss to the dark hair. He watched, dispassionately, as she carefully undid the pink blanket, touched each little toe, then each finger with what surely seemed to be solemnity. Tears glistened on her lashes, then trickled down her cheeks.

"My little girl," she said softly, and kissed the baby again.

Madonna and child, Rafe thought coldly, watching as she gently wrapped the child in the blanket, but a Madonna didn't have sex with a stranger, or deny a man the right to know he'd fathered a child—if he had fathered it.

He could accept that some women might treat sex with all the casualness of a man. The world had changed, especially in North America. Apparently, Carin Brewster was one of the new breed of female. She could tumble into bed with a stranger, enjoy the pleasure he brought her and think no more of it than if she'd shared a cup of coffee with him instead of her body.

Rafe reached for a chair, turned it around, straddled it and folded his arms along its top.

What he couldn't comprehend was why her licentiousness should bother him, or why she had decided to name him as her daughter's father.

The baby uttered a soft cry. "Hush, sweetheart," Carin murmured, and pressed another kiss to the silky curls.

If—*if*—this child were his, he would be troubled to think of a woman with such lax morals raising it. Of course, to watch her, a man would think she had all the right maternal instincts.

Rafe's mouth thinned. Was this all a performance for his benefit?

He was wealthy. Other women found that fascinating. Why wouldn't this one? She had a rich stepfather but obviously the old man didn't support her or she wouldn't have to work. She was an investment advisor, he'd learned from her sister.

"She works long, hard hours," Amanda had told him.

A child—his child, if he were foolish enough to take her word for it—could change all that.

But if that were her plan, why had she kept her pregnancy a secret?

The answer might be that she knew he'd have laughed in her face if she'd tried to trap him into a declaration of fatherhood, but fate had played into her hands. A man might be easier to convince if the woman claiming to bear his child was at the point of death.

Deus, he was exhausted, weary from two days of caffeine, anger and confusion. He'd caught only moments of sleep in the hospital waiting room. Mostly, he'd marched up and down the corridors. A hundred times, perhaps more, he'd told himself to turn around, walk out the door and never look back.

What was he doing here? he'd kept asking himself. Why had he responded to that frantic phone call from Amanda, telling him that her sister was in childbirth?

"Senhora," he'd said, his voice frigid, "this is not of interest to me. Tell it to her lover. To the man who put the child inside her."

"You are that man, *senhor.*"

"That is…" Impossible, he'd started to say, but it wasn't. He hadn't used a condom; he hadn't asked Carin if she had her own protection. Everything had happened so quickly, the shocking need to possess her, the swift rush of desire that had driven logic aside…

"My sister refused to tell us who'd made her pregnant," Amanda had said, her voice breaking.

"And now," he'd answered, while he'd tried to process the information, "now, suddenly and conveniently, she has decided to share her secret?"

Amanda had started to cry. Rafe had told himself the sobs

of Carin's sister meant nothing but the sound had torn at him until, finally, he'd closed his eyes and taken a deep breath.

"Tell me," he'd said sharply.

She told him everything, that Carin had spent long hours in labor and that, at the end, something had gone wrong.

"She's hemorrhaging," she'd whispered. "And—and, I don't know, maybe she knows she might not—might not make it, because when they let me see her, she was only half conscious…but she clutched my hand and called for you."

Rafe stirred uneasily in his chair.

That was when he'd dropped the phone and set out on a journey that he'd known might well change his life. If the child coming into the world were his, what else could he do? He was going to Carin because of the child. Only the child. It had nothing to do with her.

Could a man who had never known his own father do less?

He'd made his plans during the long flight to New York. He would ask for tests to prove his paternity: he was not a fool. But if the child were his…

What then?

Rafe got to his feet, tucked his hands into his pockets and looked at the woman with whom he'd spent the most passionate hour of his life. She was not the exquisitely groomed, expensively dressed beauty he had met that night. Her face was pale and free of makeup. There were shadows under her eyes, shadows that only emphasized her fragility. Her hair was tangled, and the plain white neckline of her hospital gown showed just above the blanket.

It didn't matter.

She would always be a woman for whom a man would abandon common sense, as he had done. Sex without protection. He'd never done such a stupid thing before, and now he was paying the price…

If she were telling the truth, and the child was his.

Rafe looked at the baby. She was beautiful. She had her mother's mop of dark hair, her widely spaced eyes, her small, straight nose but then, perhaps babies all looked like this. He had little knowledge of children. His own childhood was a dark blur, and he had been careful not to leave behind small images of himself in any of his liaisons, far more careful than his own father had been...

He dragged air into his lungs, then expelled it, told himself he had to stop thinking such things. For all he knew, the lover who'd been a ghostly presence between them that night had fathered this child.

The door swung open. A nurse he hadn't seen before flashed him the kind of professional smile he'd seen bestowed on all the new fathers on this floor.

"Hello, Daddy," she said briskly.

Rafe started to reply, thought better of it, and nodded.

"And Mommy." The woman paused at Carin's bedside. "How are we feeling?"

"Fine," Carin said, but she didn't sound fine. Her voice was shaky, and it suddenly struck him that the color in her face was too high.

The nurse seemed to think so, too.

"Uh-huh." She took the baby from Carin's arms and turned to Rafe. "Would you hold your daughter for a moment, please, sir?"

"No," Carin said quickly, "I'd rather—"

Rafe's arms closed around the baby as the nurse's hand closed around Carin's wrist.

"Let's just check your pulse. Good. Now let me just get a reading on your temp..."

"Is she ill?" Rafe asked brusquely.

"No, no, I'm sure your wife is fine."

"She is not..." He cleared his throat. It was nobody's business what their relationship was. "Perhaps she's exerted herself more than she should have."

"Mmm." The nurse read the thermometer, shot another brightly artificial smile and drew the blanket to Carin's chin.

"We need to get plenty of rest, if we're going to leave here in a few days."

"A few days?" Carin ran the tip of her tongue over her bottom lip. "Must I stay so long? I'd like to go home as soon as possible."

"You just make the most of this time, dear. Once you're home, you'll be up half the night with your baby."

Carin smiled. "Only half?" she said, and yawned.

"Of course." The nurse turned to Rafe and took the baby from his arms. "I'm sure this handsome hubby of yours will be happy to take his turn, won't you, Dad?"

"Certainly," Rafe said stiffly, and wondered just how long it would take to do the paternity test and analyze the results.

No time at all, as it turned out.

"A couple of days," the doctor told him briskly, as if new fathers asked him such questions all the time. "Less than that, I suspect, if you're willing to pay extra fees to the lab."

Rafe was willing. So was the laboratory. All that remained was for Carin to agree. He waited until her family was at dinner. Then he knocked at the door to her room.

"Yes?" she called out in a soft voice.

He opened the door, went briskly towards the bed. "We have to talk," he began...and the rest of what he'd intended to tell her caught in his throat. The baby was nursing, lying nestled in Carin's arms. Rafe caught a glimpse of her flushed face, her ivory breast, rounded and full, and swung sharply away.

"I apologize." His voice sounded rusty. He cleared his throat, spoke to the wall, told himself there was nothing in what he'd seen that should make him feel as if he'd run a hard five miles through the scrub at Rio de Ouro. "I will come back, when you are—I will come back."

He stood in the corridor, leaning against the wall, trying not to think of anything at all, but it was impossible. Images of things he'd tried so hard to forget formed in his mind.

Carin, in his arms that night. Her body, moving beneath his. Her half-stifled cries, her whispers. And now the child—perhaps, their child—at her breast, the breast he had once caressed and kissed...

He dragged his hands through his hair. He wanted a cigarette, so desperately that he could almost feel the taste of tobacco in his mouth, which was insane because he had not smoked in years.

Finally, a nurse bustled past him, went into the room and came out with the baby in her arms. Rafe stepped away from the wall, straightened his shoulders and went back inside.

Carin was sitting up in the bed, the blanket tucked around her. He decided to waste no time in telling her why he'd come.

"I've arranged for tests to be done first thing in the morning."

"Tests?"

"*Sim*. To prove the child's paternity."

Her eyes flashed. "No tests are necessary."

"They *are* necessary. Surely, you don't expect me to simply accept responsibility for your child without proof."

Why did his words hurt? She didn't want anything from him, hadn't expected anything from him.

"You're right," she said politely. "I don't expect you to accept responsibility."

"If you are afraid of the procedure, it is painless. Just a little blood, that's all."

"Dammit! Do you think that's why I...?" She took a breath, folded her hands tightly in her lap. "I'm not afraid of the test."

"Good. I will tell the laboratory—"

"But I'm not going to take it. There isn't any reason to do paternity testing."

"There is, if you expect me to acknowledge this child as my own."

"I don't expect it. Haven't you figured that out yet?"

"You sent for me, Carin."

"I didn't. Amanda seems to think I—I said your name while I was... Whatever I said, I didn't 'send' for you."

Deus, she was so calm, so self-contained. She sounded as if she deserved praise for such a thing but if the baby were his, why hadn't she sent for him? What kind of woman would want to keep a father from his child?

If she could keep her self-control, so could he.

"Nevertheless," he said, "I am here. And I intend to find out if what you claim about this child is the truth."

"I haven't claimed anything."

"Are you telling me the child is not mine?"

Carin stared at him. It would be so easy to lie...but someday her daughter would want to know the details of her birth, and she'd be entitled to the truth.

"She's my daughter," she said quietly. "I carried her in my womb. I gave birth to her."

"That's a charming speech. Unfortunately, you still haven't answered my question."

"Would you believe me if I did?" She sank back against the pillows. "Just go away," she said wearily. "I don't want anything from you."

He folded his arms, eyed her narrowly. "Not even a check each month, for child support?"

"Have I asked you for a penny?"

"How could you? You were not even going to tell me you were pregnant." His mouth twisted. "Or did you think I would be more impressed if you presented me with a child instead of a swollen belly?"

Carin flung back the blanket. He reached out a hand to stop her but she slapped it away.

"Don't touch me!" There was a white cotton robe on the chair. She reached for it, put it on, and got to her feet. "I don't need your help with anything, *senhor.* I am perfectly capable of doing things for myself. I can get out of bed. I can walk. I can do anything I damn well want, and what I want now is for you to get the hell out of my sight!''

"You can want what you like. I will do as I must. If this baby proves to be mine, I will do the right thing.''

"If she *proves* to...?'' Carin laughed, folded her arms, and faced him with her chin lifted in defiance. "Why don't I simplify things for us both, Rafe? You don't think my daughter is yours? All right. She's not.''

He had waited for those words, but what meaning did they have if they were tossed at him like stones?

"Your story changes from minute to minute,'' he said, folding his arms as she had folded hers. "I haven't come all this distance to be toyed with, Carin. I am entitled to have the proper tests done.''

God, Carin thought, how much longer did she have to tolerate this? She despised Raphael Alvares. His ego. His arrogance. His insufferable certainty that the world revolved around him.

Had she really dreamed about this man? No, she thought coldly, what she'd dreamed about was sex, and the only reason images from that night had haunted her was because it was the first time she'd felt like a woman since Frank had dumped her.

So, yes, she'd dreamed of Raphael Alvares, but that was all over. Coming face-to-face with him again, hearing him accuse her of lying, watching him as he sought ways to avoid responsibility for his very own flesh and blood, was all the proof she needed that she'd been right not to contact him.

The sooner she got him out of her life, and her baby's, the better.

"Did you hear what I said?'' Rafe clasped her shoulders. "I demand a paternity test. It is my right.''

"Your right? Your *right?*'' She laughed and wrenched free of his hands. "You have no rights. Get that through your head.''

"Your family would not agree.''

"My family doesn't make my decisions."

"Will you tell her this, when she is grown? That a man you say was her father came to you and asked you to prove his paternity, and you refused?"

"What I'll tell her," Carin said coldly, "is that she was better off not knowing you."

Rafe's eyes narrowed. "I don't have to beg for this," he said softly. "I'd prefer to do this quietly but if you refuse me…"

"I *have* refused you. You just don't want to take 'no' for an answer."

"A judge would grant me the right to such a test." He jerked his head towards the telephone. "If you don't believe me, call your stepbrother, the one who's an attorney. I'm sure he'll confirm it."

She stared at him for a long minute. Then she felt behind her for the bed, and sank down on its edge.

"Why are you doing this?" she whispered.

"I told you, I wish to do the right thing. If this child is mine, I want her raised properly. Would you deny her that?"

"I would deny her nothing. It's you I'd deny, *senhor*."

A vein began to throb in Rafe's temple. "The choice is not yours to make. This discussion is ended. I'm not asking you to take this test, I'm telling you to take it."

"Maybe that approach goes over big where you come from, but it doesn't mean a thing here." Carin got to her feet and took a step towards him, face flushed, eyes hot. "Get out," she said furiously. He didn't move, and she jabbed a finger into the middle of his chest. "Get out, dammit! Get out!"

Rafe caught her wrist, trapped her hand against his chest. "Do not point your finger at me, *senhora*. I don't like it."

"And I don't like being given commands!"

"In my country," Rafe said grimly, "women know their place."

"Oh, I'll just bet they do. Speak only when spoken to.

Walk two paces to the rear of your lord and master. And, when night comes, be sweetly compliant, in bed—'' The angry tirade caught in her throat as his gaze fell to her mouth.

"Compliant," he said, in a voice gone low and rough, "but not in bed."

Suddenly, the few inches that separated them seemed charged with electricity. The seconds dragged past and then he let go of her hand and stepped back.

"I came here because I thought you had asked for me," he said coldly.

"And if I had?" Her heart was racing, and all because of the way he'd just looked at her. Knowing it, knowing that he could still have that effect on her, made her even angrier. "What would you have done, then?"

What, indeed? He thought of how he'd dropped the phone after talking with Amanda, of how he'd run to tell his pilot to ready the plane...

"I would have done exactly what I'm doing now," he said. "I would have demanded answers."

"I've already given you answers. The fact that you don't like them is your problem."

"Why didn't you contact me, once you learned you were pregnant?"

"What for? Would you have believed me any more then than you do now?" Her eyes glittered with defiance. "I'm nothing to you, Rafe, and you're nothing to me. Let's leave it at that."

"If we created a child together, that changes the equation."

Was he right? In her heart, she knew there was validity to what he'd said.

"I—I admit, I thought about getting in touch with you, but—"

"But?"

"But..." She hesitated, remembering her shock when she'd learned she was pregnant, the one moment when she'd reached for the phone and then thought of the impossibility of telling a man she didn't know, a man who lived thousands of miles away, who had turned away from her and never looked back, that she was carrying his child. "But," she said, with a little shrug, "I decided against it. You and I—we're strangers. I couldn't imagine turning to you for help."

"Strangers who came together," he said coldly, "and made a baby. That's what you'd like me to believe, isn't it?"

"It's the truth!"

"Is it?" Rafe shrugged his shoulders, walked to the window and leaned his back against the wall. "A test will determine that."

Carin sat down on the side of the bed. She ran her hands through her hair, pushing it away from her face.

If only he hadn't come. If only Amanda hadn't sent for him. She didn't want him here, confusing things. Her life had taken a turn that had, at first, terrified her, but she'd accepted it. Once she'd felt the first flutter of life in her womb, she'd welcomed it. She'd looked ahead, planned things...

And now he was turning it all upside down...but he was right. Her baby was entitled to the same truth Rafe was seeking. She was the one being selfish this time, not he.

She looked up. "Very well," she said quietly, "I'll take your test."

He nodded slowly, his expression giving nothing away.

"I'll take your test because it's true, my daughter has the right to know the name of her father, and because I wouldn't lie about such a thing."

He gave a sharp, unpleasant laugh. "Of course you would, *querida*. You are a woman accustomed to her freedom, and now you have an unplanned child in your life. What will happen to that life, if you have to spend your days working and your nights at home, rocking a cradle?" His lips drew back from his teeth in a predatory grin. "We both know I can change all of that."

Carin lay back against the pillows. The robe fell open; she

saw his eyes drop to her breasts, full and rounded with milk, to the softly clinging cotton gown that covered them. She wanted to drag the robe closed but she knew that would somehow give him the advantage. Instead, she brought the lapels together slowly, as if she were alone.

"You're wrong. About everything."

"Really." Rafe tucked his hands into his pockets and walked slowly towards her. "How am I wrong?"

"I don't live the kind of life you seem to think I do. And I have a job. A career. It pays me well."

"You mean, you had a career."

"Excuse me?"

"You are a mother now."

"So?"

"So, your career is ended."

Carin laughed. It was the first time she'd really laughed in longer than she could remember and it felt good.

"Excuse me, *senhor,* but perhaps no one's pointed it out to you yet. This is the twenty-first century. Women work and raise children at the same time. I'm sure that's news to you, but—"

"Women who must, do so. Women who have a choice, do not."

Her chin lifted. "Then it's a good thing I have a choice."

"Your confidence is amusing, *querida.*" He paused beside the bed. "But then, you are confident about everything. About this child, for instance."

"I don't believe it," she said wearily. "Are we back to that? I said I'd take your test…"

"I was only with you the one time. Do you know what the odds are of becoming pregnant from such an encounter?" A muscle flickered in his jaw. "You came to me from another man's bed. You will regret it, I promise you, if this is the child of your lover and you're trying to use me, once again, to do what you wish he would do."

"I hate you," Carin whispered. Tears rose in her eyes and

she brushed them away with the back of her hand. "Damn you, Rafe, I *hate* you!"

"That isn't what you told me that night," he said coldly, "not while I was deep inside you."

His head dipped to hers; he kissed her, his mouth crushing hers, his fingers tangling in her hair and tilting her face up to his. She made a soft sound, half protest and half something that might have been surrender. It drove his blood straight to his groin and he pulled back, hating himself, hating her, hating whatever cruel twist of fate it was that had brought them together.

"You—you bastard!"

He thought of telling her that she was right, that he was exactly what she'd called him, and that he was here only because he would see to it that his child—if this were his child—would carry his name, but she had no need to know such a personal thing about him.

"I carried her in my womb." Carin's voice shook with emotion. "I gave her life, almost at the cost of my own. And I'll make the choices that will define her life. You'd better accept—"

"We come from different worlds, *querida.* In yours, morality is a game. In mine, women know their place. Men rule their homes, their lives, and their women."

"How unfortunate for the women."

He laughed, but the sound was flat and cold. "So you may think now, *minha dona,* but if the test results prove that I am, indeed, the father of your child, you will learn that there are advantages to such a life." His gaze dipped to her lips, then lifted and met hers. "An obedient woman has nothing to worry about. She is well cared for."

"So is my neighbor's cat, but none of the women I know would choose to trade places with her."

"Ah. But, you see, that is an excellent analogy. A cat learns its place, learns to obey simple commands and stay close to home, and it is rewarded. It's stroked and petted. It's given baubles and gifts. And, if it is very, very good, it's permitted to spend its nights in its master's bed.''

Carin felt a chill race along her skin. ''What are you talking about? What does any of this have to do with me, or with my daughter?''

Rafe smiled. Carin watched the curl of his lips, the flatness of his eyes, and suddenly a chasm seemed to open before her.

''It's late.'' Her voice sounded thin and reedy and she cleared her throat. ''Please leave now, Rafe. I'm very tired.''

He could see that she was. Her skin was so pale it seemed translucent; there was a fine tremor to her mouth. He imagined taking her in his arms, not to make love to her but to hold her close and soothe her, which only proved how good she was at making a man blind to reality.

The rest of what he had to tell her could wait until after the tests—if the tests showed that she was telling the truth.

''*Sim.* Rest, by all means. You will leave the hospital soon and once you do, your life will change. It's best you prepare for it.''

''Of course my life will change,'' she said quickly. ''I know that. And I'm ready for it.''

Rafe paused, his hand on the door knob. Slowly, he turned and looked at her. ''I hope so, *querida*,'' he said softly. ''But, somehow, I doubt it.''

CHAPTER FIVE

NEW YORK had been enjoying a warm, sunny Spring but the weather took a sudden change.

It was raining on the morning Carin was to be discharged from the hospital. The gray downpour suited her mood as she sat in a chair across from a representative from Bio Tech Labs. The rep had brought her the results of the tests she, Rafe and the baby had taken.

Rafe was her child's father.

Carin had known what to expect but seeing the information that would affect three lives printed out in stark black letters sent an emotional shockwave reverberating through her system.

She tried not to show what she was feeling but she knew she wasn't doing a very good job of it because the rep paused in the middle of a sentence.

"Are you all right, Ms. Brewster?" the woman asked. "Shall I send for the nurse?"

Carin shook her head. "No. No, I'm fine. It's just—all the rain… It's cool today, isn't it?"

"Yes," the tech said, "it is," but the look in her eyes said she'd seen it all before, the disbelief in a woman's face when she read words that confirmed what she already knew, that the last man on earth she wanted to deal with was the father of her child.

When Carin thought she could speak and not have her voice quaver, she folded the report, carefully inserted it back into its envelope and held it out. The Bio Tech rep shook her head.

"Oh, no, Ms. Brewster. That's your copy. Keep it, please.

Now, before I leave, is there anything you didn't understand, or you'd like me to explain?''

Yes, Carin thought. How could one night's mindless passion lead to such a mess? Not to the birth of her daughter. Already, with her baby not a week old, she knew how much she adored her. The thing she didn't comprehend was how Rafe had suddenly become a part of her life.

In the blink of an eye, he'd gone from being a stranger to being a man demanding participation in her child's future. It didn't matter that she wanted nothing from him, that she'd have given anything to banish him from her world. He had plans that somehow made hers secondary. Like it or not, she was going to have to deal with him.

"Ms. Brewster?"

Carin looked up.

"Do you have any questions for me?"

"No. None, thanks. The report is—it's very clear."

"Yes, well, we pride ourselves on clarity." The woman shut her briefcase, got to her feet and held out her hand. "The best of luck to you, then. We hope that our services have been of help."

"Thank you." Carin shook the woman's hand, watched as she walked to the door. "Actually—actually there is one thing…"

"Yes?"

"Has Senhor Alvares received a copy of the report, too?"

"Certainly. Yesterday, in fact. It was too late to bring it to you but he'd requested the information as soon as—"

"Thank you. I understand."

Except, she didn't.

The door swung shut. Carin stared at the report lying in her lap. If Rafe had seen the proof he'd demanded, why hadn't she heard from him? He'd been so filled with stiff-necked speeches about responsibility and obligation. Was the reality more than he could accept? Until the end, he must have clung to the hope that Frank was her baby's father.

Carin bit back a moan. If only she could go back in time, change things, not have called out for him...

The baby, lying in a small portable crib next to her chair, made a soft sound in her sleep. Carin reached into the crib and gently touched one tiny hand.

"Not you, dumpling," she said softly. "I wouldn't change you for the world...but your father is a different story. I wish I didn't have to deal with him."

But she did.

Rafe's arrogance infuriated her; his refusal to believe that he'd made her pregnant insulted her. And the way he'd looked at her last night, when he'd talked about changes in her life, terrified her.

What did he know that she didn't? He'd insisted on proof that he was her baby's father. Okay, he had that now, along with his name on the birth certificate. She hadn't waited for the paternity report; she'd known what the results would be and last night, she'd instructed the hospital to list him as "father." She'd also named her baby.

Her daughter would be called Amy.

"Amy," Carin said softly, and took the baby from the crib just as Marta Baron walked briskly into the room.

"Oh, that's lovely," Marta said, beaming happily at her daughter and granddaughter. "Amy. Such a charming, old-fashioned name. Does Rafe like it?"

"I have no idea." Carin's voice was cool. "I didn't consult him. It isn't his business."

"Now, sweetie, I know you're angry at him, but—"

"Angry? At a man who demanded a test before he'd acknowledge he's my baby's father?" Carin laughed as she rose to her feet. "That's not really the right word, Mother. Which reminds me...the results are in." Her voice hardened. "Rafe has the proof he wanted. He's Amy's father."

"Well, of course he is," Marta cooed, as she reached for Amy. "Hello, precious. And how is my lovely little girl this morning?"

"She's fine, and she wants to go home. So do I."

"Not yet, sweetie. We have to—to wait. For—for the nurse." Marta smiled brightly. "You can't just walk out of a hospital. They have to take you out, in a wheelchair."

"I don't need a wheelchair," Carin said, and hated herself for sounding like a spoiled twelve-year-old. "I'm perfectly capable of walking."

"Don't be so impatient. Besides, I promised Rafe…" Marta caught her lip between her teeth. "I'll go find the nurse."

"Wait a minute." Carin grasped her mother's arm. "What did you promise Rafe? And when did you talk to him?"

"Oh…" Marta waved her hand in the air. "A while ago."

"He's here? In the hospital?"

"No. Not yet…" Marta flushed. "Oh, dear, I'm saying too much!"

"You aren't saying enough. What's going on?"

"Nothing."

It was such a transparent lie that Carin would have laughed, except for her mother's refusal to look her in the eye.

"Mom," she said softly, "what aren't you telling me? What could you and Rafe possibly have to talk about?"

"For goodness' sake, Carin, don't be like that. The man is the father of your child."

"Thanks to temporary insanity," Carin said coldly.

"He's determined to do the right thing for your child, and for you."

"Oh, sure. That's why he hasn't even called to apologize for saying I lied, for believing I'd been with Frank when he was the only…" Carin took a deep breath. "This is silly. What Raphael Alvares believes is his affair. Please, let's go now."

"All I'm asking you to do is to be fair, darling. To yourself, to the baby…and to Rafe."

"I don't believe this. Are you going to defend him?"

"Well, I do think you could have been more open with us, Carin. Why you let us think that the two of you had just spent that one night together…"

Carin stared at Marta, who fell silent. Had everybody gone crazy?

"What are you talking about, Mom? It *was* only one night. Why would I make that up, if it wasn't true? I don't know what fairy tale Rafe's told you, or why, but—"

"I told her everything, *querida,* as I should have, from the beginning. It is the best thing to do, for us all."

Carin swung around. Rafe stood framed in the open doorway. He was wearing a snug black T-shirt, faded jeans and scuffed black leather boots, and he had an enormous bouquet of bright yellow roses in his arms.

He looked incredibly handsome; his smile almost looked real and for a heart-stopping moment, she thought of how it would have been if he'd known about Amy all along, if he were here to gather them both in his arms and take them home…

"*Bom dia, Marta.*"

"Good morning to you, too, Rafe."

Marta smiled as he took her hand and brought it to his lips. A look passed between them, one Carin couldn't figure out. It made her feel like an outsider… An uneasy outsider.

"And Carin." He turned to her, his dark eyes sweeping her in quick appraisal and she felt a quick stab of anger because he'd suddenly made her aware of how she must look. She hadn't bothered with makeup, and the dress she'd put on strained across her too full breasts and still-rounded belly. "And *bom dia* to you, as well, *querida.*"

"Rafe," she said carefully.

"You have seen the test reports."

It was a statement, not a question. She angled her chin up a notch. "Yes."

"Good." The corners of his mouth lifted in a smile. "This is a very special day for us both."

"It certainly is. I'm going home. And you're getting your surname on Amy's birth certificate."

"Amy?"

"Yes. Why do you look surprised? Surely, you didn't expect me to go on referring to her as 'my baby,''' Carin said with a tight smile.

"Our baby," Rafe said quietly. "And I only wonder, didn't it occur to you to discuss the choice of a name with me?"

"Why would it? You wanted to be acknowledged as her father and I've accommodated you, but all other decisions are mine."

"Are they," he said, though it seemed anything but a question, and then he dipped his head in agreement. "Very well, *querida*. Amy it shall be." He smiled, and she could see the steel behind the smile. "I like the name, so it is no problem."

She thought of telling him the only problem lay in his arrogance but what was the point in arguing with him? Soon, mercifully soon, Rafe Alvares would be out of her life.

"Actually, 'Amy' could be thought of as a shorter version of a name I have always loved. Amalia."

Carin smiled brightly. "I'm sure that some woman in your past would be delighted by that news. Frankly, I don't care what you love or don't love. Your tastes are of no interest to me."

"Carin." Marta cleared her throat. "Darling, Raphael is only saying—"

"He's saying far too much. He's not going to be raising Amy. I am."

"Ah. Well, I know that's what you... I mean, that's how it... Rafe? Don't you—don't you want to tell Carin something? I really think—I think you should."

Carin stared at her mother. Marta was worrying her upper lip with her teeth. She was never easily disconcerted but she was now.

"Tell me what?" Carin said warily. Rafe had gotten his way. Amy carried his name. What more could he possibly want? Visitation rights? Maybe he'd contacted an attorney. She'd been afraid of that, concerned about getting involved in a lawsuit with a man whose resources would be endless.

"Marta," Rafe said, though his eyes never left Carin's, "would you leave us, please?"

"Oh. Oh, of course. I just… Carin? Darling, I know you're still angry but please, try and think of the baby. And of how much you and Rafe cared for each other before all this happened."

"What are you talking about? We didn't—"

"Marta."

Rafe spoke softly, but the single word resonated in the room. Carin felt a sudden clenching in her gut, one that grew more intense when her mother threw her a nervous smile and hurried from the room with Amy in her arms.

Rafe closed the door, turned and folded his arms, and she knew something terrible was going to happen.

"What's going on?" she said in a shaky voice. "How did my mother come to this amazing conclusion, that you and I have some sort of—of history?"

"She was distressed by the terms of our relationship." He smiled lazily, though the smile never reached his eyes. "I simply did what I could to alleviate her concerns."

"We don't have a relationship."

"We created a child. I know you would prefer not to acknowledge my role in that, *querida,* but it is a fact."

"Let's not argue over who didn't want to acknowledge what. Just tell me what you told my mother."

He shrugged again, hooked his thumbs into the belt loops of his jeans and came slowly towards her. Her heart banged into her throat. She wanted to back away but she wouldn't give him the satisfaction.

"I told her that it was true we'd met that night, at Espada, for the very first time." He reached out, slid his hand against her cheek. She tried to turn away from his touch but he rested his thumb against her cheekbone, slid his fingers into her hair. "And then I added some details, to make everything else more acceptable."

"What details?"

His hand was soft against her skin, his fingers gentle as they combed through her hair. Memories flooded through her. He had touched her like this on that night. Gently, at first, then with power and hunger...

"What details?" she repeated sharply, and she took the step back she'd promised herself not to take. "Stop doing that."

He smiled, closed the distance between them. The foot of the bed hit the backs of her legs; she was trapped.

"I like to touch you," he said softly. He bent his head, breathed in her scent. "All these months, I remembered how good it was to feel the softness of your skin under my hands and mouth."

Carin clenched her hands at her sides. She remembered, too, but she would never admit that to him. Never.

"Answer my question. What did you tell Marta?"

Rafe took her face in his hands. "I said that we met that night, at Espada, for the very first time." His gaze fell to her mouth, then lifted. "I didn't say it, but I permitted her to think that we were intimate that night."

"You permitted her to..." Carin gave a hollow laugh. "Anyone who can count from August to May can figure that out for themselves."

"What they cannot figure out, *querida,* is that we saw each other many times after that, in New York."

She blinked. "What?"

"I said—"

"I heard what you said, but it's a lie." She clasped his wrists, tried to keep him from sliding his fingers into her hair. "You never saw me again, Rafe. You never even saw me that morning, at Espada. You had left, without a word."

His gaze flattened. He let go of her, stepped back and tucked his hands into his pockets.

"Perhaps you noticed my absence even before that, when you finally unlocked the bathroom door," he said coldly. "Is that your usual behavior with your lovers?" His smile was quick and unpleasant. "Surely, it's not the way you treated the love of your life."

"Who?"

"Your Frank. I cannot imagine you put a bolted door between you, after a night spent in his arms."

Frank had never made her feel vulnerable enough to want to bolt a door, she almost said, but that was another admission she'd never make to this man.

"You can't be foolish enough to think there's any comparison between the things I did with Frank and the things I did with you, can you?" He didn't move but she saw a slight tightening around his mouth. Good, she thought bitterly. She'd hit Rafe Alvares right where he lived. "And it isn't Frank we're talking about, it's you, and the nonsense you fed my mother. Did you think she'd feel better if she believed we'd seen each other in New York? I've had a child out of wedlock, Rafe. I know it may not matter to lots of people in today's world, but—"

"It matters to me. And it matters to your family. That's why I offered a more palatable story to your mother."

"Thank you so much." Carin's words were cold with sarcasm. "It's nice to know you're the thoughtful type."

"Listen to me," Rafe snapped. "And pay attention, *querida,* so that there are no discrepancies in our stories." His eyes darkened and locked on hers. "I told her that we saw each other many times, that we were much drawn to each other but that we had a lovers' quarrel, before we knew of your pregnancy, and that we parted."

"I don't know why you bothered with such an elaborate lie. I'm sure it pleased her to think we were lovers instead of—"

"It pleased everyone, or so it would seem." A thin smile curved his mouth. "We have had messages offering good wishes from your stepbrothers, and from Nicholas and Amanda. Did you know they left for Paris yesterday?"

"Yes. I know. Amanda stopped by here, and... Good wishes?" Carin shook her head in confusion. "For what? Did my mother pass along that ridiculous fairy tale? I can't believe anybody in my family would fall for it."

"Ah, but they did." Rafe's smile was slow and intimate; so was the touch of his hands as he cupped her shoulders. "Perhaps you come from a family of romantics and they'd prefer imagining you in a marriage based on love, and not on necessity." He read the shock in her eyes and his smile tilted. "That's right, *querida*. I explained to Marta that we intend to marry."

His words stunned her. Married? To Raphael Alvares? She knew he didn't mean it, that he'd invented a story to ease the situation, but even thinking about such a thing, imagining herself as his wife...

"You shouldn't have done that!" Carin moistened her lips with the tip of her tongue. "It's only going to make things more difficult."

"I disagree."

"She'll nag me, now. She'll want to know when we're getting married."

"She won't ask," he said, very softly.

Slowly, carefully, he undid the top two buttons of her dress, slipped his hands inside, cupped her naked shoulders. She caught her breath, told her heart to stop banging like a drum.

"She will. You don't know my mother. She'll ask, and ask, and—"

"There will be no need, *querida*, because I have already answered the question. You and I are to marry today."

Carin felt the blood drain from her head. She swayed; Rafe's hands tightened on her.

"Is this supposed to be funny? Because it isn't. And I resent your lying to my mother about something like this. When she finds out the truth—"

"She already knows the truth. You are to be my wife."

"You're definitely not funny, you're crazy." She twisted away from him, took a quick step back and closed the buttons with trembling fingers. "I am not going to be your anything!"

"I've made all the arrangements."

"You've made all the…" Carin laughed. "You really are crazy, *senhor!*" She reached behind her, snatched a sweater from the bed. "You need a stay in this place more than I ever did. I think the psychiatric department is on the top floor. Just check with the nurse, as you go—"

He caught her by the arm as she started past him. "You think this is a joke, Carin?" His mouth thinned; anger flashed in his eyes. "It is not. I have the license."

"You can't get a license by yourself," she said stupidly.

Rafe laughed. "You can, if you have the right contacts."

He was serious. Crazy, but serious. Calm down, she told herself, just calm down.

"Maybe. But you need more than a license." She jerked her arm free of his hand. "You need a warm, willing body. You can't marry a woman who refuses to marry you. Not in the United States. Women aren't property. My mother could have told you that."

"Your mother," he said coldly, "thinks that this is all wonderfully exciting. She knows how happy this news will make you." His teeth glittered in a quick, tight smile. "You will tell her that it has."

"Forget it. I'll tell her the truth. And, once I have—"

"I have more than our marriage license, *querida.* I also have all the documents I need to take my daughter home, to Brazil."

Carin had started towards the door. She froze, then turned and looked at him.

"I don't believe you. Proceedings like that take a long time. Months, even years..."

She fell silent. Rafe was holding a sheaf of papers in his outstretched hand.

"Take a look. Here are the custody papers, and here is her passport. And please, do not waste my time telling me what one can and cannot do, in the United States." His eyes lanced into hers. "I have friends. Powerful friends. By the time you manage to get the documents you'll need to stop me, my child and I will be on Brazilian soil."

"*My* child," Carin answered, her voice trembling.

"Our child, if you use your head and do the only intelligent thing."

She stared at him for a long moment, hating him, hating herself, hating the hour of unbridled passion that had put her at his mercy.

"You have no right to do this to me," she whispered.

"I have the right to see to it my child grows up properly."

"You wanted her to have your name. I gave it to her."

"That does not make her legitimate."

Carin laughed. "My God, just listen to you! Talking about legitimacy in one breath and blackmail in another."

Rafe looked at his watch. "Make a decision, please. The official who will marry us is already waiting at my hotel."

"Rafe." Carin shuddered. It had been cold in here before. Now, she could almost feel her blood turning to ice. "Rafe, listen to me. You want access to my daughter? You can have it. I'll give you visitation rights. You can see my child—"

"Our child. Why is that so difficult for you to say?"

"Our child." She swallowed dryly, fought to keep her head. "Yours, and mine. We'll work something out. A plan—"

"The hour grows late, Carin." He spoke brusquely; his face might have been carved from stone. "I told my pilot to have my plane ready by noon."

"Your plane?"

"It is a long flight to Brazil, but do not worry, *querida.* I have spoken with your doctor and I've carried out all his recommendations for your comfort."

"For my…" Carin reached behind her, felt for the bed and sank down on the edge. "Rafe. At least give me time to think. Just—just put things off until tomorrow…"

She lifted her face to him and he saw how pale it was, saw how her eyes had turned into bottomless pools of darkness and the memory came to him, unbidden and unwanted, of how she had lifted her face to him that night, of how deep and dark her eyes had seemed as he'd possessed her.

And then he remembered the rest of it, how she had used him, how she had rebuffed him, how she had tried to pretend he *had* no child, and his heart hardened.

His daughter was all that mattered.

He held out his hand, his face expressionless. "We're wasting time. Are you coming with me, to tell your mother our good news?"

"But—but my home is here. My life is here."

"Your life is with me now. In my country." He gave her a thin smile. "You will be Amy's mother, and my wife. An obedient, dutiful wife, who shares my bed and never looks at another man, nor breaks the vow of fidelity."

"I'll never share your bed, you son of a bitch! Do you hear me? Never. Nev—"

Rafe lifted her to her feet, gathered her into his arms and kissed her, moving his mouth against hers until her lips softened, parted, clung, however unwillingly, to his.

"Querida," he whispered, *"querida,* do you see how it can be, between us?"

She pulled back, breathing hard, and stared at him through eyes gone dark and blind.

"What I see," she said, her voice trembling as much with anguish as with the depths of the lie, "is that I can pretend you're Frank. Is that what you want? For me to go to your bed, shut my eyes and imagine another man, moving inside me?''

He didn't think, he reacted. He drew his hand back, saw her flinch but hold her ground...

No. *Deus*, no. He dropped his hand to his side. He had never struck a woman. She wasn't going to reduce him to the kind of man who did, no matter how she tormented him.

"The child is all that matters. Get that through your head, my soon-to-be wife. I will do anything for Amy and if you are wise, you will not get in my way." Without warning, he swung her into his arms. "Your mother says it is hospital policy for you to be escorted from the premises when you are discharged, Carin. But I am the only escort you will need or want, from this moment on."

CHAPTER SIX

SIX weeks later, Rafe stood in the tall grass alongside his private airstrip in southeastern Brazil and watched as his plane lifted into the sky.

The jet was taking Carin's physician and his nurse back to New York. Rafe had flown them to his ranch for his wife's post-partum checkup. Carin had refused to see the specialist his own doctor had recommended. She'd said she preferred to fly to the States to be examined by her own gynecologist but Rafe was not a fool. He suspected she'd have found an excuse to stay in New York, once she was there, so he'd arranged for Dr. Ronald to come to her here, at Rio de Ouro, instead.

"Your wife is fine," the doctor had just told him. "She's completely recovered. Life can go back to normal."

He'd offered Rafe a quick man-to-man smile. Rafe knew what the smile meant but it was not anyone's business that he had no intention of being his wife's husband in anything but name only.

The jet gained altitude quickly and headed towards the Sierra Gaúcha mountains that separated the endless prairie from the ocean. He watched until it was out of view, then touched his stirrups to his horse's sides and headed back to the house, and to his office. One of his men ran up and took the horse's reins from him as Rafe dismounted. He nodded his thanks, automatically slapped the dust from his jeans and went across the patio and into his office.

It was cool inside the house, thanks to high ceilings and slowly revolving fans that cast gentle shadows on the pale cream walls as they stirred life into the torpid air. Rafe drew the chair from his desk, sat down, turned on his computer and began reviewing the records of the last six weeks.

Rio de Ouro was doing well, just as it had been ever since he'd bought the ranch a dozen years ago. His cattle grew fat on the grass of the pampas. His horses had some of the world's finest bloodlines. And away from the ranch, his varied interests in São Paulo and Rio de Janeiro were successful beyond anything he'd ever imagined.

"Whatever you touch turns to gold," Claudia had told him once.

Rafe frowned. That was true, if you judged success by the number on the bottom line of an accounting statement. But if you judged it by his relationship with his wife...

What did that have to do with anything? He had a child he loved, one who would grow up with two parents. That had been his goal, and he had achieved it. Someday, Amy would ride this land beside him and love it as much as he did. His frown eased away; his lips curved in a smile. Surely, a man could not be faulted for taking pleasure from seeing his dreams come to fruition.

After almost an hour, Rafe signed off the files and shut down the computer. He swiveled his chair around so that he was facing the glass doors that led to the patio, tilted back, laced his hands behind his head and let his thoughts drift down the long road he had traveled to get to this time and this place.

Sometimes, even now, he could hardly believe it. He'd almost told that to Carin the night he'd brought her here.

"Where are we?" she'd murmured, her voice husky with sleep as she stirred in his arms.

He'd been holding her ever since she'd begun tossing in her sleep. The nurse he'd hired to accompany them to Brazil had reached for her medical bag.

"Your wife is restless," she'd said. "I'll calm her with a sedative."

My wife, Rafe had thought. He'd watched as the woman

took a hypodermic syringe from the bag. "No," he'd said quickly, "she doesn't need that."

Then he'd reached for Carin. She'd gone into his arms with a soft sigh, quieting right away, looping an arm lightly around his neck and laying her head against his shoulder, the way she had the night they met. Rafe had gathered her close against him, feeling not the hot tug of desire in his belly but a sudden fierce protectiveness.

His wife didn't need a sedative. She needed the feel of a man's arms around her.

His arms.

He'd held her that way for hours, even after his shoulder began to cramp, telling himself that he was only doing it because it was right. Eventually, he'd dozed off, too, his face against her sweet-smelling hair, his body warm with the heat of hers. And he had dreamed.

He'd dreamed that his bride smiled as he carried her over the threshold of his house; that she came to him in the darkness, dressed in a long gown of sheerest white lace, and pressed her open mouth to his; that she awoke in his arms to tell him how happy she was to be home with him, in the place he'd built with his own hands.

And then he'd awakened, to find Carin stirring in his arms as the plane kissed the ground, to hear her say, "Where are we?" in a tone that implied the answer might well be that he had taken her into the bowels of Hell or the darkest side of the moon.

Rafe rose from his chair and paced to the patio doors.

He knew she hated it here. She hadn't said it but she said hardly anything to him. Still, he could tell how she felt about Rio de Ouro. It was in her eyes, as she looked out across the endless *pampas,* in the set of her shoulders as she made her way through the house...but then, he hadn't expected her to love it. He had brought her here against her wishes. She despised the ranch, the house...

She despised him.

It didn't matter. He had done what he'd known he must do, for his daughter. As for the ranch—why should he care what Carin thought? He loved it. That was sufficient. He had always loved this place, even before he'd laid eyes on it. This land had been part of him, of his dream, for as long as he could remember.

He had grown up on his mother's bedtime descriptions of the ranch. Her vision of it, anyway, because she had never seen it, either. His mother had been a dancer in a nightclub in Rio when she met his father, and though Eduardo da Silva had never deigned to bring his mistress to his home, he'd described it to her.

She, in turn, had described it to her son, even long after da Silva had left, even when he was nothing but a memory. She'd told Rafe about the big house, the outbuildings, the endless prairie and the rugged mountains.

Amalia Alvares had given her child a dream.

When Rafe was twelve, his mother died. Of poverty, of despair, of what happens to women who lose their youth and their beauty, and have nothing else to sustain them.

Rafe lived on the streets and on his wits until he was fourteen. One morning, kicked awake by a policeman, cold and hungry but mostly filled with anger at the mother who'd died and left him and the father who'd never acknowledged him, he'd decided to take his destiny into his own hands.

Deus, how could he have been so naive? Skinny, dirty, hiding his fear under a layer of street-smart toughness acquired hustling *touristes* on the beach at Copacabana, he'd set off for the paradise his mother had described, and for the father he'd never seen.

It had taken him weeks to cover the distance between Rio de Janeiro and the endless prairies and mountains of Rio Grande Do Sul. He hitched rides on carts and in wheezing old trucks, walked until his feet were blistered, begged for food and stole it when his belly was so empty it growled, and slept wherever he could.

Why was he doing this? he'd asked himself, as the miles slipped past.

He'd been sure he knew the answer. He was going to confront the man who was his father.

Rafe took a bright red apple from a silver bowl, tossed it up and caught it. Then he pushed open the patio doors. A rush of afternoon heat enveloped him; he stepped outside, slid the doors closed, and walked slowly to the iron railing that enclosed the patio.

If he'd had a plan beyond that, he couldn't recall it. Curse Eduardo da Silva? Tell him that the woman he'd once claimed to love was dead? Beat him until he begged for mercy?

Rafe smiled thinly, tossed the apple again and propped one booted foot against the base of the railing.

In the end, he'd done none of that. His long journey ended at a ranch in a state of ruin. Parched land, a handful of bony cows and tired horses. Outbuildings on the verge of collapse, a house with holes in the roof...and an old man, sick, dying, and pitiful.

Rafe had left the place within hours.

Eight years later, he came back. He had lived a lifetime in those years, learning to read and to write, to think with his head and not with his heart and fists. Best of all, he was rich, his pockets filled with the gold he'd panned for in a river hidden deep in the jungle.

And Rio de Ouro, even sadder-looking than before, was for sale.

Rafe sold his gold, put half the money into investments nobody but he believed in, and sank the rest into the purchase of the ranch. To this day, he could recall the sly look on the face of the agent who'd sold it to him.

"You have made an excellent buy, *senhor*," he'd said, even though his smile said Rafe was a fool.

"I believe I have," Rafe had replied politely, and he'd meant it.

He'd gone into the small towns that clung to the foot of the Sierra Gaúcha, to the rougher towns scattered over the *pampas,* searching for men who were not afraid of hard work. Together, they'd torn down what remained of the da Silva house and built a new one. It was not a dark, Spanish-style fortress like his father's but a house made of glass and tile, open to the sun, the wind, and the beauty of the land.

They built stables and barns and fences. They burned scrub. And Rafe worked as hard as his men, even after the investments others had sneered at turned into the first of his millions. When a man created his own private world, he wanted his sweat and blood, his pain and his joy, to be part of it.

Time passed. He moved in circles of wealth and power, and he began thinking about the future, and about passing on all he had built. When he met Claudia, things seemed to fall into place. She was charming and beautiful, and came from an old Brazilian family. He assumed she understood the importance of continuity, but the only things she understood were parties and jewels and herself.

He knew they were not right for each other, and he ended their engagement, vowing to be more careful next time.

He'd choose a woman who would cherish the world he'd built.

Rafe stood straight and gazed blindly towards the mountains.

Instead, he had made one mistake, and now he had a wife who was even less suitable than Claudia would have been, and who despised him and the life to which he'd brought her.

But he had a child. That was what mattered. Someday, everything he'd built would be Amalia's. That was how he thought of Amy, as his Amalia.

It was amazing, the games fate played. He had taken a woman to bed, unthinkingly planted a seed in her womb, and she had given him a daughter that she named Amy, unknowingly choosing the diminutive form of his mother's name.

He'd thought of telling that to Carin but he suspected she'd have begun calling the baby something else if she knew the name pleased him and had a connection to him, so he said nothing. But he took joy in whispering "Amalia" to his little girl when he held her, and to know that she carried the name of the woman who'd given him life, and who had worked herself into an early grave because the man who'd fathered him had turned his back on them both.

An insect chorus set up a loud trill. Rafe scowled into the hot afternoon and it seemed to get the message. Silence descended on the patio, and the stretch of waving grass beyond.

Yes, he had a daughter he adored…and a wife who was as much a stranger to him as she had been the night he'd taken her to bed, almost a year ago. After six weeks of marriage, all he really knew about Carin was that she liked to visit with his horses and that she hated the sight of him. She wasn't subtle about it, either. *Deus,* there were times she went out of her way to let him know how she felt.

"Raphael," she would say, if their paths crossed on the stairs or on the grounds.

Then she'd tilt her head and sail on past him as if he were invisible, or as if he were a servant—except, she didn't treat the servants that way. He'd come into the kitchen early one morning and found her talking with the cook or trying to, anyway, stumbling over a sentence half in Portuguese, half in English, laughing until she saw him. Her laughter had died and she'd given him that imperious nod as she swept by.

She talked with the baby's nanny, too. Really talked, because he'd hired someone who spoke English as well as Portuguese. More than once, he'd heard the sound of their voices and their laughter drifting down the hallway towards his rooms.

She never so much as smiled when she spoke to him.

"Are you well?" he would say.

"Yes," she'd reply.

"Did the things I ordered for the baby suit you?" he'd ask.

"They did," she'd answer.

"Do you need anything? Would you like me to take you to São Paulo or Rio, so you can shop?"

No, no, and no.

João, who spoke perhaps six sentences on a good day, was a better conversationalist than his wife. That was bad enough when they were alone but on several occasions in the last few weeks, he'd had visitors. His banker. His accountant. An old friend, who'd heard he'd married and had stopped by, unannounced, to say "hello."

In each instance, Carin had appeared only after he'd sent for her.

"Hello," she'd said politely, "how nice to meet you."

Then she sat in a chair—not beside him, on the sofa, but in a chair on the opposite side of the room—and she'd said nothing, done nothing, not rung to ask the maid to serve coffee, not inquired if his guests wished a drink or something to eat. She'd simply sat there, a polite smile on her face, until he'd wanted to storm across the room, drag her to her feet, shake her, shout at her, kiss her until she came to life and heat lightning flashed in those cool eyes of hers...

Rafe sucked in his breath.

No. Hell, no. He didn't want to kiss her. Why would he? Despite what he'd told her the day he'd married her, he'd reached a decision. She was, she would always be, his wife in name only.

The night he'd carried her into his home, he'd thought of taking her up the stairs, to his room, to his bed...not to make love to her, because he was not a monster, no matter what his bride believed. He knew she needed time to heal from the rigors of childbirth, but a man's wife belonged in his bed.

Marrying for the sake of a child was the right thing to do, but only a fool would live with a woman—a beautiful woman—without enjoying her.

And then he'd looked down into Carin's face. She was staring at him as if he *were* a monster, her eyes icy pools of darkness against the pale translucency of her skin, and a sense of self-loathing had roiled through him, like the water of the Amazon in flood.

He'd said nothing, only carried her to one of the guest suites and left her there, and that was where she'd made her life over the past weeks, in her own rooms or in the nursery, or anywhere at all where she would not have the misfortune to cross paths with him.

He knew he had only to command her to move into his rooms and she would have no choice but to do so. In his country, unlike hers, he held all the power in their marriage. But he wouldn't do it. It was what she expected of him, and he would not do it.

In fact, he didn't want his wife in his bed anymore.

He was a Brazilian; he lived in a country in which men didn't have to apologize for their needs. Mistresses were commonplace, especially among those of his class and wealth. He'd taken them before. Soon, he'd take one again. The simple truth was, he no longer wanted Carin sexually. She held no interest for him, except as the mother of his child.

He'd come within a second of telling that to her doctor, when the man had offered that little smile with the news that Carin was well.

"I've told her she may resume intimate relations with you," the *medico* had said, with some delicacy, when Rafe didn't respond to the smile.

Rafe had nodded. "I see," he'd said.

Had there been something in his voice that had given him away? He wondered about it, because the doctor had flashed him a look of understanding.

"You must realize, *senhor,* that, ah, that such things may require a little patience. Some women take longer than others to recover from the experience of a difficult childbirth..."

Rafe opened the patio gate, closed it after him, and began walking towards the stables.

The difficulty of childbirth had nothing to do with his wife's distaste for him but he didn't care. All he wanted now was that she assume her proper role, as his wife. He would tell her, tonight, that she could no longer ignore him. She would dine when he did, preside over his table, entertain his guests, grace his arm at public and private functions.

He would tell her, too, that he did not require her to lie in his bed. She could erase that from her mind.

Perhaps he would turn to Claudia to soothe his sexual needs. She had been shocked to learn he was married—she'd phoned a week ago, and he'd told her, though, of course, he'd given no details.

"I'll miss you, darling," she'd said, as if they'd still had a personal relationship—but they could. For all her faults, Claudia had never disappointed him in bed. She'd also made it clear that she'd be happy to be there again, if he asked. He never had, but now…

Why not? he thought, as he reached the paddock where the stallion he'd bought from Jonas Baron kicked up its heels in the sunlight. Claudia was beautiful, and she would not need to pretend he was someone else in order to moan with ecstasy in his arms. Her only complaint about him had been that she meant less to him than Rio de Ouro.

"You love this desolate place more than you could ever love a woman," she'd said when he'd ended their engagement. "It's the only thing you ever think about."

Rafe sighed.

It was close to the truth, but marrying Claudia would have been a mistake had he never set eyes on the ranch. She was a spoiled little rich girl; he'd grown weary of her games, of her self-indulgence, of her unfaithfulness. In his culture, the law often looked the other way if a man beat his woman, even killed her, for infidelity, but he'd simply told Claudia he no longer wished to marry her.

She'd accused him of never losing control enough to raise a hand to her because his real passion would always be for his land and never for a woman.

He thought back to that moment in Carin's hospital room. She'd taunted him by saying she'd have to pretend he was Frank before she could lie in his arms again.

He had raised his hand, then. It was the first time he'd ever come close to such a thing, but it had nothing to do with passion for Carin. It was because she was impossible.

She made him crazy.

Deus, she was making him crazy again, and under his own roof. Well, that was done with. He no longer felt desire for her but she had a role to fulfill. She was his wife. His commands were to be obeyed.

Rafe whistled softly to the stallion. The horse pricked its ears and looked at him. He opened his hand so it could see the shiny red apple on his palm. The stallion tossed its head and trotted to the fence. Rafe smiled and rewarded its behavior by giving it the fruit.

The horse had been difficult, when he'd first brought it to the ranch. It had been headstrong, almost wild, but, with patience, he had changed that. Now, the stallion came when he called it; it no longer nipped his fingers. Simple training had worked wonders. Good behavior warranted a reward. Bad behavior warranted none.

Rafe rubbed the horse's ears. Women were not so different, when you came down to it. They could learn, the same as horses.

Carin would learn, too.

If she wanted her life to continue as it had gone these last weeks, if she wanted her own rooms, her privacy, then she would learn to come when called, smile when required, dine at his table if he had guests, and carry on a civilized conversation. She would treat him with respect in private, with deference in public, cling to his arm if he demanded it. She would say the right things and pretend she was happy.

If she didn't behave, there were ways to bring her to heel.

He could fire the nanny who spoke American English, tell the grooms his wife was not permitted to visit with his horses, demand she give up the room she slept in, alone, and force her to share his room, his meals, his bed...

His bed.

Rafe stepped back from the fence.

What was he thinking? He didn't want Carin in his bed. Even if he did—and he didn't—since when was that a method he would use, to get her there?

Behave yourself, or I'll take you to bed. I'll take off your clothes, slowly, until you're writhing in my arms; I'll make you stand before me while I kiss my way down your body and when I reach that sweet, secret place between your thighs, I'll open you with my fingers, taste the bud that flowers there, torment you until you clutch my hair, cry out my name, beg me to lay you back on the bed and sheathe myself deep, deep inside you...

Deus.

He was hard as stone. And it was crazy, because he didn't want Carin, didn't desire her, didn't...

Hoofbeats thundered towards him. He stared in disbelief as his wife rode past on a stallion so huge it dwarfed her. Carin's dark hair flew behind her; she was laughing, bent low over the horse's neck as she rode into the narrow, cobbled courtyard that separated the two wings of the stables. The animal snorted and obeyed when she pulled back on the reins, though it still danced impatiently as Rafe ran towards it.

"Are you insane?" he shouted, and grabbed the bridle. "Do you have any idea of the power of this stallion?"

The horse whinnied nervously and tried to toss its head. Rafe tightened his hold.

"Get down!"

His wife's smile disappeared and she shot him a look filled with loathing. "Don't you dare speak to me that way."

"I'll speak to you any way I please, dammit. Get off that horse!"

Carin threw her leg over the pommel. One of the grooms had come hurrying into the courtyard. Rafe handed him the reins and reached for his wife. She tried to bat his hands away but he ignored her and lifted her from the saddle. She kicked hard as he lowered her to the ground; one boot caught him just below the knee and he grunted with pain but he didn't let go. Instead, he manacled her wrists with his hand.

"Who saddled this beast for you?"

"That's none of your damn business."

"Ricardo?" Rafe looked at the groom, who was cowering against the horse. "Was it you?"

In his rage, he spoke in English but the boy seemed to understand. He nodded his head in mute misery.

"Collect your things," Rafe snarled. "Tell João to give you your pay. You're fired!"

"It's not the boy's fault," Carin said, as she struggled to free herself of Rafe's grasp. "I chose this horse. I told him to saddle it."

"He should have known not to do anything you asked. I am his master, not you."

"What you are is a savage and a brute. And I hate you!"

Rafe smiled through his teeth. "That is not news, *senhora*, nor does it distress me. Hate me all you wish but it will not change the facts. I am your husband. If you wish to ride, you must first ask my permission."

He knew he sounded like a monster but he didn't give a damn. This was his wife. She had ignored him, made a fool of him, tormented him long enough. *Deus*, she might have hurt herself. Killed herself. She could be lying in his arms, broken and bloodied...

Rafe took a deep breath.

"Ricardo!"

The groom looked at him. *"Sim, senhor?"*

"You are not fired. Take this animal and cool it down.

And remember, I am the only one who gives orders around here.''

"You—you bastard," Carin hissed. "You no good son of a—"

Rafe had had enough. He mouthed an obscenity, picked up his wife and tossed her over his shoulder. Carin shrieked in fury.

"Put me down!" Her fists pounded, hard, against his back. "Damn you, Rafe! Put—me—down!"

He strode up the hill, towards the house. He could hear his breath whistling because he was breathing hard but it was because of anger, not because of his wife's weight. She was light. Too light, he thought furiously; wasn't she eating properly? The doctor had said she was fine but what did he know? Nothing, for clearly, he had not forbidden her to ride a horse.

"You are not well enough to ride," he said grimly, as he banged open the massive front door and marched through the big tiled foyer, then up the stairs. "Didn't the doctor tell you that?"

"I specifically asked him if I could ride," Carin panted, as Rafe kicked open the door to her bedroom. "He said I could."

"The man is an idiot. *You* are an idiot. Or didn't you tell him your plan was to ride an elephant?"

"For God's sake... Oof!" The air rushed from her lungs as Rafe dropped her on the bed. "You're making a mountain out of a molehill. I can ride. I've been riding since I was a little girl. The doctor gave me a clean bill of health. I..." Carin's eyes widened. "What do you think you're doing?"

"What does it look like I'm doing?" he said coldly, as he ripped her clothes from the closet and tossed them on the floor. "Elena? João! Where in hell is everyone?"

His roar echoed from the walls. His housekeeper rushed into the room. She stared at Carin, who sat against the headboard of the bed, then averted her eyes as if the sight were too awful to watch.

"Sim, Senhor Raphael?"

Rafe swung towards her, legs planted apart, hands on his hips. He looked wild and angry, and Carin's heart lurched at the sight of him.

"Find João. Have him help you move all my wife's things to my rooms."

"No," Carin said quickly. "Elena. You are to leave my things right where they are."

"Didn't you understand what I said before, Carin?" Rafe stalked to the foot of the bed and glared at her. "I am master here." He jabbed his thumb against his chest. "I make the rules. You are my wife, and I am tired of playing games. Elena!"

"Sim, senhor."

"You will have the *senhora*'s things moved by dinnertime. Is that understood?"

The housekeeper shot a quick look at Carin, then nodded. *"Sim."*

"And you will plan a meal appropriate for a small dinner party, for tonight."

"Oh, that's it," Carin said. She sat up straight and folded her arms. "Celebrate my humiliation with a party. What are you going to do with me while you and your pals are laughing it up, huh? Chain me to a wall?"

"Six people," Rafe said, ignoring her outburst. "The *senhora*, myself…" He paused. "I shall decide on the other four. Yes, that sounds fine." He turned to Carin, a cold smile angling across his mouth. "Don't you agree, wife?"

Carin swung her legs to the floor. "What I agree is that you've lost your mind. I am not attending a dinner party, not unless you're being served up as the centerpiece. You want to have a party? Fine. Have one. Elena?"

"Sim, senhora?"

"I will have my dinner here, in my room. Actually, in my sitting room." Carin addressed the trembling Elena, but her eyes never left Rafe's. "Something light, please. A salad, some iced coffee..."

"Prosciutto with melon," Rafe said. "Then prawns with that sauce I like so much. Tell João to bring up some of that French white wine from the cellar." He turned a polite smile on Carin. "Drinks at eight, I think. How does that sound? And dinner at nine, on the patio."

"Dinner in hell, you son of a—"

"Thank you, Elena. That will be all."

The housekeeper scurried from the room. Carin glared at Rafe.

"I don't like prawns. I hate white wine. I never eat melon. And any guests of yours will automatically be enemies of mine."

He folded his arms. "Are you done?"

"For the moment."

"In that case, I'd suggest you pay attention. I don't like repeating myself." He smiled tightly. "You will bathe and put on perfume. You will dress in something long and feminine. And you will join me, at a few minutes of eight, so that we are ready to greet our guests together. It is time I introduced you to my friends."

"I'm not the least bit interested in meeting them."

"Throughout the evening," Rafe said, as if she hadn't interrupted him, "you will smile at me and say the sort of things a woman says to her husband. My guests are not to be treated to your sharp North American tongue."

Carin lifted her chin. The simple action made his breath catch. She was still filled with defiance, and it only added to her beauty.

"Didn't you hear me? I don't want to meet your friends."

"You will do as you are told."

"I will not! You may have had the power to force me into this marriage, to bring me here, to this—this godawful corner of the earth where you play at being emperor, but you can't force me to pretend I like it." She swung her legs to the

carpet and stood up. "I am not your property. I am not...
What's so damned funny?"

He came towards her, smiling. When he reached her, he
took her shoulders in his hands, drew her unyielding body
forward.

"That was a fine performance, *querida*. Truly, it was excellent. But you are wrong. I can do whatever I wish with
you. You are my wife. My property."

"That's nonsense."

She spoke sharply but her voice shook. Good. It was time
she feared him. All these weeks, watching her waltz through
his home as if it were a hotel, as if she were visiting royalty
and he was a servant...

"You're trying to scare me, Rafe, but I'm not a fool. This
is a civilized country. It has laws."

"Indeed, but the laws are very different than they are in
your country." His eyes dropped to her mouth, then rose to
meet hers. "I thought I would let things go on as they have
been," he said, "that we would live in this house together,
as strangers."

"We *are* strangers. We have nothing in com—"

He kissed her before she could finish the sentence, his
mouth gentle against hers despite the anger of the past few
minutes. When she would have turned her head away, he
clasped it between his hands and went on kissing her, until
she sighed against his mouth.

"I could take you by force, *querida*, but I won't."

She let out a breath. "Then—then why—"

"Husbands and wives should not sleep apart."

"I have no intention of sleeping with you, Rafe."

"You will sleep in my arms tonight, even if that is all you
do. But I promise you, *querida*, there will be more, and it
will be because you come to me of your own choice."

She gave an unsteady laugh.

"You find that amusing?"

"I find it amazing, that you should even think—"

He lowered his head, kissed her mouth again, with slow deliberation, until he felt the first, faint tremor slide through her body, heard the whisper of her first, soft moan. Then he tilted her face up, slipped the tip of his tongue between her lips, coaxing them open. He waited until she sighed and gave him access to the honeyed warmth of her mouth, until her hands rose to clasp his wrists.

Then, as much as it killed him to do it, he let go of her and stepped back.

"You said we have nothing in common, *querida,* but we do. It isn't what either of us would wish, perhaps, but it's more than many people have." He looked at her, then ran his hand down her cheek, to her throat, to her breast, and she took a shuddering breath as he cupped her flesh. "You will beg me to take you, Carin. I promise you that."

"I won't," she said in a shaky whisper. "I swear it, Rafe. You'll wait forever before that happens."

He smiled, lowered his head and kissed the pulse that raced in the soft hollow of her throat.

"Until tonight, *minha mulher,*" he said softly.

It took every bit of his control to leave her there, and walk out the door.

CHAPTER SEVEN

CARIN stood in the center of her bedroom and watched as Elena and João emptied it of the last of her possessions.

At first, she'd tried to stop them. "Don't do this," she'd said. "You don't have to obey the orders of a barbarian."

She'd spoken in English, which she was sure João understood, even if he pretended he didn't, but she knew it didn't matter, that neither he nor the housekeeper needed to understand her words to get the message.

Elena's face was flushed. She cast a couple of seemingly apologetic glances in Carin's direction, as if to say she regretted her role in this but what could she do, except obey?

"The master has spoken," Carin said bitterly. She flung herself into a chair and folded her arms. She had never felt so helpless, or so angry, not even when she'd realized she'd been nothing but a one-night stand for the man who was now her husband.

The housekeeper and the houseman shuttled back and forth until, finally, João stopped in the doorway with Elena just behind him. João made a stiff little bow.

"Senhora."

If ever Carin had heard a one-word speech, this was it. He was telling her that he and Elena had completed the job. As if she couldn't see that for herself, Carin thought grimly. The closet stood wide open, stripped of everything that had hung there. The bureau drawers were empty. The bathroom vanity no longer held her toiletries and cosmetics.

There wasn't a sign she'd ever occupied this room that had been her sanctuary.

She looked up at João, who still stood in the doorway, his face expressionless, his arms at his sides, as if he were wait-

98

ing for his next command. Did he expect her to thank him for a job well done? Was he waiting to be dismissed?

That was a laugh. Rafe had just made it clear that she had no rights in this house, that she was nothing but property, like his horses and his land. Now, his servant was waiting for her to send him on his way.

She rose to her feet, thumbed her hair behind her ears, stood as straight and tall as she could when, inside, she was trembling with rage.

"Go," she said. "Just—just get out of here."

The houseman gave her another stiff bow and did as she'd asked. Elena lingered a second longer, her hands knotted together at her waist. She looked as if she wanted to say something but what was there to say, after The Great God Alvares had spoken?

"It's all right," Carin said wearily. "Really, it is."

"He is good man," Elena said softly. "He has kind..." She searched for the word, then thumped her chest. "He is kind in here, *sim?*"

The housekeeper gave her a wan smile and hurried from the room.

Rafe, a good man with a kind heart? There was no explaining some things. For all Carin knew, someone might have said as much about the Roman emperor Caligula. She felt like laughing but she sensed that if she let any sort of emotion show right now, she'd never be able to keep it under control.

Anyway, there was no point in wasting time laughing or crying or feeling sorry for herself. Giving in to emotion wouldn't change a thing. She'd figured that out weeks ago, during that endless flight from New York, when she'd sat staring out the window as the world she knew slipped away from her. Her thoughts had chased after each other like rats in a maze until, finally, she'd let fear and exhaustion drag her into a dream-tormented sleep...

Sleep that had become soothing and peaceful when she'd suddenly felt herself cocooned in the warmth of Rafe's arms.

Carin walked to the window, stared out at the flat prairie and the distant mountains.

Why had he held her all those hours? And why had she let him do it? It wasn't as if she hadn't known she was curled in his arms. She'd come awake long enough for that, to feel the strength of his embrace, the heat of his body, the steadying beat of his heart.

Tell him to let go of you, she'd thought, but it had been so good, to be in his embrace. The lights in the plane had been dimmed, there'd been no sensation of motion, only the moon and the stars lighting the heavens as Rafe took her from her old life to a new one. She'd waited for the terror to rise up again and choke her but it hadn't. What she'd felt, instead, was a hot excitement at the knowledge that she was Rafe's wife, that she belonged to him now, that he would not leave her again...

Carin swung away from the window and strode from the room.

Maybe she was married to a crazy man. How else to explain why he could be so tender one moment and so unfeeling the next? Maybe *she* was crazy, for even trying to make sense out of it, but she was a captive in this house, in this marriage, trapped until she could somehow force Rafe to see that the life he'd planned couldn't possibly work, that he couldn't expect to create a happy little family by chaining the members together.

The French porcelain clock in the upstairs hall struck six. Drinks at eight, wasn't that what he'd said? Drinks at eight, dinner at nine. She was to bathe, dress in something long and feminine, come down to greet his guests and behave like the perfect wife. At evening's end, he would permit her to sleep in his bed. And someday soon, he was certain, she'd crawl to him on her belly, begging to be petted like a favored house cat.

"In your dreams, *senhor*," she said coldly.

His suite of rooms was at the other end of the house. Her heart was pounding by the time she reached the door. She raised her hand to knock, but she didn't. If she was to share his space, she would not come to him like a supplicant. She took a deep breath, hoped the butterflies in her stomach wouldn't turn into a swarm, and opened the door.

She stood in the entrance to a sitting room. And it was empty.

Carin shut the door and sagged back against it. Bravado could only carry you just so far, and hers had vanished. Her knees seemed to be made of rubber as she surveyed the emperor's lair. Breathe in, she told herself as she walked towards a doorway that she knew would lead to the bedroom. Breathe out. And whatever you do, don't look at the bed... But how could she avoid looking at it? It would probably be covered in black satin, it would fill the center of the room, there'd be mirrors in the ceiling above it...

She laughed.

It was just a bed.

Oversize, yes, but that was all. No mirrors, no black satin, just a handsome four-poster covered with a white duvet and heaped with pillows. The bed faced a wall of glass that looked out on an enclosed terrace lush with potted plants and shrubs.

There was a mirrored wall to her left. There was a wall just like it in one of the Baron guest rooms; she knew the mirrors would hide a dressing room that led to a bathroom and shower. Yes, there was the latch.

Carin slid the doors open. Rafe's clothes hung neatly in an alcove on the left...and there were her things, hanging on the opposite side.

The butterflies in her stomach fluttered their wings and rose in a whirling cluster. There was a disturbing intimacy to seeing her clothing and his, together. She knew it was dumb to feel that way. Dressing rooms were dressing rooms, nothing more…

Except, this dressing room was Rafe's. And he was her husband.

Carin slid the door shut. "Stop it," she said under her breath. Bluebeard had been somebody's husband, too. Being a "husband" didn't make a man a good guy. Rafe certainly wasn't. He was a cold-hearted dictator, who thought he owned her.

Well, he didn't.

He could never own her, no matter what he believed.

She took a steadying breath and opened the mirrored door again. Rafe's cool, commanding voice rang in her head. Bathe, he'd said, as if she wouldn't have known enough to do that unless he ordered it. Put on perfume. Wear something long and feminine.

Long and feminine, indeed.

He was going to put her on display tonight, for his friends. She knew what sort of woman they'd expect, at least, she could take a pretty good guess. *Dona* Alvares would be a credit to her husband's good taste. She'd be perfectly groomed, elegantly gowned and coiffed, docile and well-behaved. Her every smile would make it clear that her only purpose in life was to please her master.

Rafe's wife would be a cat, she thought, with a taut smile, just as he'd suggested. A creature who lived to be stroked and petted, and to spend its nights in its master's bed.

Carin slapped her hands on her hips. "Cats have claws, *senhor*," she said, as if Rafe were standing in front of her. "You seem to have forgotten that."

A cat with claws would not follow orders. Long and feminine, indeed, she thought grimly, as she ran her eye over the garments hanging before her. No, not the black silk. Not the red one, either. Impatiently, she pawed through her dresses. Any one of them would have suited her would-be master, but that was all the more reason they wouldn't suit her... What was this? She'd never owned anything like this soft rose silk, or this slender bit of silver...

Carin's breath caught.

These were the things Rafe had bought for her. She'd forgotten that he'd done that, or maybe it was more honest to say she'd studiously ignored it. The first couple of weeks after he'd brought her to Rio de Ouro, boxes and packages had arrived with stunning regularity, all of them bearing her name, but as soon as she'd realized what they'd contained, she'd stopped opening them.

"I don't want anything my husband buys me," she'd told Elena. "Give the stuff away. Burn it. Do whatever you like, do you understand?"

It was obvious Elena hadn't done that. Instead, she'd tucked his gifts here, in Rafe's dressing room. Now, for the first time, Carin saw all the things he'd bought for her.

They were beautiful. Soft silks. Iridescent satins. Butter-soft cashmeres.

She touched her hand to the rose gown, then to the shimmering column of silver. The colors, the cuts, were perfect. She'd have selected them herself, if she'd been Cinderella with a fortune at her disposal. The silver gown, especially.

How terrible would it be just to look?

She slid the gown from its hanger, held it against her body, looked into the mirror and sighed with pleasure. Oh, it was exquisite, simple and low-cut, with thin straps and a long, narrow skirt.

Carin put one hand into her hair, swept it high on top of her head. Yes, she'd do it just like that, with a couple of strands tumbling loose around her cheeks and maybe at the nape of her neck.

Her eyelids drooped. She imagined leaving the bedroom, going slowly downstairs, to Rafe. His eyes would darken when he saw her; he'd hold out his hand and she'd take it, entwine her fingers with his.

"Querida," he'd say, not mockingly but with tightly-

controlled passion, and she'd smile and lift her face for his kiss, and as the kiss deepened he'd lift her into his arms and carry her back up the stairs, here, to his room, to his bed...

"No!"

The word burst from her throat. She tossed the silver gown on the floor, pushed all the rest of the clothes Rafe had bought her aside...

And found what she would wear tonight.

The lime-green nightmare she was supposed to have worn for Frank and Iris's wedding.

She waited to feel something, anything, a stab of pain or a rush of anger, but she felt nothing. It was as if all of that had happened to someone else, not to her.

Iris had sent her that note, asking her to pass the gown on. She hadn't. She remembered standing in her bedroom, reading the note, then looking at the gown.

"I bought it," she'd said grimly. "I paid for it. And I'm going to have the pleasure of shredding it into a million pieces of shiny polyester..."

But she'd forgotten all about it and now, here it was, packed by Marta or whoever had come in to empty her apartment and send her clothing to her, the stereotypical bridesmaid's dress that people joked about.

Actually, it was worse than that. It was, plain and simple, a horror. Not her color, not her style. It was the ugliest piece of clothing she'd ever owned.

She took the gown from its hanger, held it against her body and looked into the mirror. The color was hideous, made even worse by gold ruffles at the neck and hem, and by the unhealthy shine of the fabric. There were dyed-to-match shoes, too, clumsy things with stubby heels and long, pointed toes.

Iris had loved it. She'd dragged her into the *Beautiful Brides* shop at the mall, gushing about the perfect dresses she'd found for her attendants.

"Isn't this stunning?" she'd said, and Carin had finally said well, well, it certainly was unusual...

"Unusual" was the word.

What had Rafe commanded? Long and feminine. That's what he wanted, so he could exhibit his conquest properly.

She smiled. The gown was long, and Iris had thought it was feminine.

"Don't ask for something unless you're sure you know what it is you're going to get, *senhor*," Carin said softly.

She laid the gown on the bed, put the shoes on the carpet, locked the door and began to prepare for her debut as *Dona* Alvares.

For a man who was all ego, it was going to be a very long night.

At seven, Carin stepped from the shower. The tub had been tempting but what was the sense of taking a bath in something so big and beautiful if you didn't dump in some beads of bath oil? And she wasn't going to do that.

She wasn't readying herself for a party, she thought coldly, she was readying herself for revenge.

She wrapped herself in an oversize towel, padded, barefoot, through ankle-deep carpeting to the bedroom...and turned rigid with shock, at the sound of someone at the door. Heart pounding, clutching the towel, she swung towards it. The knob was turning but that was all it was doing. The lock held.

"Carin?"

Rafe. Of course. How had she managed to forget that he'd expect to shower and dress, too? Her heart went into overdrive.

"Yes?" she said, hoping she sounded cool and unconcerned.

"Unlock the door."

No "please." No "would you kindly." Just words spoken

as a command. She straightened her shoulders, pushed her wet hair back from her face and glared at the door.

"No."

Silence. Not even the doorknob rattled. She could almost envision the look on Rafe's face at finding himself locked out of his domain.

"Our guests will be here soon."

"Your guests, not mine."

"Dammit, Carin, open this door!"

She smiled. It was lovely, hearing that harsh note of disbelief in his voice. "Sorry," she said, and did her very best to make sure he could tell that she wasn't in the least bit sorry. "I'm getting dressed. That's what you told me to do, remember?"

"I did not tell you to lock me out of my own rooms." He spoke softly, as if he were only inches from the door but then, he wouldn't want João or Elena to witness him being defied by this insignificant creature, this woman he'd forced into a sham of a marriage. "Open this door at once."

The door seemed to vibrate under the sudden weight of his fist. Carin took a quick step back. She was wrong. He didn't care if his servants knew she'd locked him out of his rooms.

What if he got angry enough to break the door down? She imagined the wood splintering, Rafe bursting into the room, tearing the towel from her hands...

A shimmering wave of heat swept through her body as she imagined him reaching for her, his anger fading to something else as he bent her back over his arm and kissed her until she whispered his name, until she clung to him...

Oh, God.

"No! I'm not opening the door, Rafe, until I'm ready to come downstairs."

An eternity crawled by before he spoke again, this time in a purring whisper.

"You're playing with fire, *querida*. I would advise you to remember that those who play with fire can get burned."

"And I would advise *you* to find somewhere else to get ready for the evening."

"I could break this door down."

"Yes." Her voice trembled. "Yes, you could, and then we'd both know that you really are a barbarian."

She heard him let out a long, heavy breath. "You wish to behave like a spoiled brat? Do so—but only for tonight. I will not permit this again, *minha mulher*. Do you understand?"

She understood, all right. He wasn't a monster, not by his reckoning, anyway. That was why he hadn't touched her during the past weeks. But he wasn't a man with a conscience, either. As of tonight, the rules had changed.

Unbidden, certainly unwanted, that sweet, liquid heat thickened her blood again.

"Yes," she said, "I understand."

She sank down on the bed as his footsteps receded. She was still shaking moments later, when Elena tapped on the door. Carin opened it and the housekeeper murmured words that were surely apologetic as she went quickly through the room, collecting Rafe's things. A white dinner jacket. Black trousers. A black silk T-shirt. Her husband was going to look gorgeous tonight...

But he wasn't her husband, Carin reminded herself quickly. He was the enemy.

Elena shut the bureau drawer. "*Senhora*," she said politely...and froze. She stared at the hideous lime-green gown draped across the bed, then looked at Carin with a stricken expression on her face.

Carin sighed. "I know," she said, even though she wasn't sure Elena understood the words, "but he deserves it."

Oh, yes, she thought, as she locked the door again. It was going to be an interesting evening, and even more interesting to see if Rafe thought the prize was worth the game after she finished with him.

At five of eight, Carin stood before the mirror.

She looked awful.

Some dresses improved when you put them on. Not this one. If anything, it was uglier. Since she'd come to the ranch, her skin had taken on a soft golden hue. The shiny green fabric turned the golden tan a sickly yellow.

It was a bad shade for her hair, too. She'd deliberately not blown it dry or even brushed it out; it hung straight and lank, which was bad enough, but the color of the gown leached out all the highlights so that she looked as if she'd dipped her head in a bucket of dark brown paint.

Carin bit her lip, turned sideways and stared at her reflection.

She'd filled out, after having Amy. It wasn't something she liked to admit, even to herself, but a couple of times she'd caught herself glancing in the mirror as she dressed in the morning, wondering if Rafe remembered her body as it had been and what he would think of it now, with fuller breasts and more gently rounded hips. Not that she cared. Not that she'd ever give him the chance to see it…but she'd wondered.

Filled out? She blew out a breath. Maybe that was an understatement. She didn't just look fuller or rounder in this dress, she looked like a sausage.

Did she want Rafe to see her like this?

He was so handsome, her husband. So gorgeously masculine. He could have any woman he wanted, and he had chosen her…

She stiffened.

That wasn't true. He hadn't chosen her. Circumstance had done the choosing. If she hadn't become pregnant with his child, if he didn't have some—some crazy sense of Latin morality, she'd never have seen him again.

And it hurt, to know that. Oh, it hurt. In the dark hours of the night, she lay awake in her bed, alone, thinking of what it would have been like if Rafe had come to her, come for her, because he wanted her. Because he needed her, loved her...

A moan of despair burst from her lips. She spun away from the mirror, her hand at her throat. What in hell was she thinking? Rafe didn't need her or love her, and she didn't need or love him. He just thought he owned her but after tonight, he'd know better.

She strode into the bathroom. Elena, or perhaps João, had carefully placed her cosmetics on one end of the huge marble vanity. She opened half a dozen tubes and jars, then slapped something from each on her face. A lipstick she'd gotten as a giveaway and hated came next, and then so much mascara that her lashes stuck together in clumps.

She stepped back and took an appraising look at herself.

"Lovely," she whispered and then, before her courage failed her, she shut off the lights, walked through the bedroom, unlocked the door and stepped into the hall. Soft music and the purr of voices drifted up the stairs.

Rafe's guests had arrived.

Who would he have invited to dinner? Local people, almost certainly; who else could get here on such short notice? Neighboring ranchers, the kind Jonas enjoyed and Marta tolerated. Rawboned men would sip bourbon, chew their cigars and talk about horses and cows while pleasant women with sun-leathered skin exchanged the latest gossip.

And all through the evening, she'd sit demurely beside Rafe in her hideous gown and overdone makeup, with her hands neatly folded in her lap, saying nothing, doing nothing, being the demure little woman while his neighbors tried to figure out why a man like him, a man who could surely have any woman he wanted, would have taken such an unattractive wife.

Laughter wafted towards her again, a mix of deep masculine and delicate female tones. Nothing about the sound suggested cigars or leathery skin. Butterflies took wing in Carin's belly once more but this time, they swooped and darted.

Was this plan to humiliate Rafe really such a good idea?

It wasn't too late to scrub her face, brush her hair, change from this awful gown into something else, something silky and soft that would make him smile with pleasure when he saw her, turn his eyes dark with desire as they had that first night...

She stopped, swallowed hard, took a couple of calming breaths. That night was long gone. Rafe had made her pregnant, she'd given him a child, and that was the only reason he'd returned to her, forced her into a marriage she didn't want, a marriage he thought gave him the right to turn her into a slave.

Carin's eyes narrowed. She flipped the ruffles at the neckline of her gown, smoothed down the skirt and started down the stairs.

She didn't need Rafe, she didn't love him, and she certainly didn't want to stay married to him. With any luck at all, he wouldn't want to stay married to her, either.

Not after tonight.

CHAPTER EIGHT

WHERE was Carin?

Rafe took a drink of wine and glanced at his watch. It was well after eight and everyone was here—the da Sousas, who were his closest neighbors, and Claudia and her latest lover who, as it turned out, were visiting with Isabela and Luiz for the weekend.

Only his wife was missing.

"Where is she, darling?" Claudia had asked in English the second she came in the door.

"Making herself beautiful for her new husband," the gentleman with her had replied.

"I'm sure she's beautiful enough, as it is. A man like Rafe wouldn't settle for anything less," Isabela had joked, and everyone had laughed.

Everyone was speaking in English in deference to Carin—but where the hell was she? Rafe knew it was ridiculous to be on edge. He'd come up with the idea of this dinner more out of anger than anything else, but this really was the first time any of his friends were going to meet his wife.

His wife. Just thinking those words gave him a strange feeling.

Rafe lifted his glass to his lips again. Claudia said something and gave a trill of laughter. He smiled, too, even though he hadn't heard a word she'd said. He couldn't get his thoughts on anything but Carin, and how it would feel to put his arm around her, feel her body fit the curve of his and introduce her.

This is my wife, he would say, and Claudia and her lover, Isabela and Luiz would all see that the woman he'd married was even more beautiful than they'd imagined.

111

Beautiful, and hot-tempered, and furious at him. But he would change all that, later tonight. After his guests left, he would kiss Carin until her anger turned to passion and then, at last, he truly would make her his wife...

"...still can't get used to the fact that you're married, darling," Claudia said, putting her hand on his arm. "My Rafe, with a sweet little *mulher*."

Sweet? Rafe almost laughed. "Prickly" was a better word for his wife.

Dammit, what was keeping her?

Claudia sighed dramatically. "Oh, well. I'll just have to wait until you get tired of this one and come back to me."

It was an old line. She'd used it for years. He'd always smiled and taken it as a joke but for some reason it was annoying the hell out of him tonight. And why did she persist in calling him "darling"? That had never irritated him, either, but tonight it grated on his nerves.

"I don't intend to get tired of this one," he said, as lightly as he could manage. "Carin and I are married, Claudia. I explained that when you telephoned."

"*Sim,* so you did." She smiled, smoothed the lapel of his white dinner jacket. "You are married, and you have a child. How quickly you work, darling Raphael."

Rafe frowned into his wineglass. Maybe it hadn't been such a clever idea, inviting his former fiancée to dinner, but he'd arranged this party on such short notice that there hadn't been time to do much planning. Besides, all he wanted was to be sure Carin believed him when he said it was time she stopped pretending their marriage was a game. She had to enter into his life, accept her role as his wife...

Her role, in his bed.

An image of her, naked in his arms, flashed before him. Desire, sharp and electric as lightning, sizzled through his blood.

What was wrong with him? He had guests, Claudia was

talking to him, and all he could think about was bedding Carin.

"…listening to me, darling? Rafe, you're hurting my feelings."

He blinked, forced his attention to Claudia, who was looking up at him from beneath her lashes. She was flirting with him like crazy. Well, she always did; it was part of her and it didn't bother her that her lover was standing ten feet away, or that his wife was about to join them…

Deus! What an idiot he was. He'd told his former fiancée about his wife, but he had not told his wife about his former fiancée. And, of course, he should have. Women were difficult creatures to understand at best, but he could see that it would not be pleasant for a bride to learn her husband had once intended to marry another woman by coming face-to-face with that woman, with no warning.

Well, it was too late, now, just as it was too late to call this off. What had he been thinking, to make so many changes in one day? He'd moved Carin into his rooms, told her it was time they had a real marriage, and now he was about to introduce her to Claudia.

His jaw tightened.

The fault was hers, as much as his. Carin should not have made him so angry. What sort of man would *not* get angry, if his wife made it brutally clear she refused to think of him as her husband?

"…fly to São Paulo next week, darling? We could have dinner and…"

Claudia walked her fingers down his arm. He caught her wrist and held on. It was the only method he could think of to keep her from touching him again.

And, dammit, he was *still* angry. Was this any way for a wife to treat a husband? For her to show him respect? If Carin didn't appear soon, he'd go upstairs and get her, even if it meant breaking down the door she'd locked against him.

How dare she lock him out of his own rooms? How dare she treat him with such condescension?

His hand tightened around the wineglass.

All of that was done with, now. She would do what was expected of her. She would look beautiful, behave demurely, speak when spoken to and charm his guests. And later, when they were alone, he would lock the bedroom door against the world and show her—and show her...

Rafe lifted his glass to his lips and drained it.

What would he show her? That he had a frightening lack of control where she was concerned? That she could enrage him with a cold look? That he had never stopped wanting her in his arms again?

Tudo bem. All right. Memory had turned a simple act of sex into something too intense to be real. Taking Carin to bed would get things back to normal.

"Rafe?"

Damned right, it would. A wife was meant to sleep with her husband. It was time to teach her that. And, after tonight, she would think of no man but him. He would take her until she was exhausted, until her body ached from his possession. He would make her his, drive the man she had loved, might still love, from her body, her heart, her soul...

"Rafe," Claudia said again. "Oh, my goodness..." Soft laughter bubbled from her lips.

"Pare!" Isabela hissed, and Claudia's laughter did stop, but too late. Rafe could feel the hair rising on the back of his neck. His guests were all staring past his shoulder.

"What is it?" he said, and turned around...

And saw his wife, dressed like a bad joke in a fashion magazine.

She stood in the arched entrance to the living room. He thought, at first, she was ill, because her skin seemed so yellow. Then he realized it was the color of her gown that made it seem that way. *Deus,* the gown was a green so bright it hurt his eyes. It was shiny, too. If a fabric could be said to have a radioactive glow, this one surely did.

The gown didn't fit right, either. It was tight, but not in the way snug garments could flatter a woman. It pulled at the seams, making doughy lumps of Carin's lush curves. What were those things at her neck and ankles? Ruffles? Rafe stared, horrified, at the woman who was his wife. He had never imagined her in ruffles. She was too slender, too elegant...at least, she had been, until tonight.

And her hair. What had she done to turn it from silk to straw, to make it a flat brown instead of rich chocolate?

Rafe took a shuddering breath. Surely, this was a bad dream, or some hideous North American joke.

"Rafe," she said, and smiled.

His hand tightened on his glass. Her mouth was painted a deadly shade of purple; she had a smear of the stuff across one front tooth.

"Rafe, please forgive me. I'm so sorry I'm late."

She didn't even sound like herself but like a combined parody of Marilyn Monroe and a world-weary Jessica Rabbit. And why was she begging his forgiveness? The Carin he knew would never beg for anything.

Deus, what had happened? He had sent the doctor away too quickly, and clearly she needed his services. Wasn't there such a thing as post-partum depression? *Sim.* There was. The wife of a friend had suffered from it. Perhaps this—this psychosis was one of its manifestations. Was this his fault? Had he pushed too hard, frightened her into trying too hard to please him?

Claudia tittered again, and he flashed her a furious look. Isabela whispered something to her husband, her voice gentle. It was good she was here. She'd had children. Surely, she would know how to deal with...

"Rafe," Carin said softly, and something in the way she spoke his name froze his blood. He looked away from the terrible gown, the hideous shoes, the purple mouth, looked into her eyes...

White-hot rage exploded deep inside him. For a moment, his mind went blank.

His wife's eyes were not filled with pleading, or teary with depression. They glittered, hard as stone, with cold, sharp, malice.

She had done this deliberately.

He wanted to kill her.

No, not that. Killing was too easy. What he wanted to do was throw his guests out the door, grab Carin and shake her until her purple-smeared teeth rattled, until those hideous ruffles danced, until she really did beg and plead for mercy. Then, only then, he would rip that ugly gown from her body, tear off his own clothes, take her, right here, on the floor, until she knew that he was her master, that he would not tolerate such behavior.

He took a deep, deep breath, then glanced around the room. Isabela da Sousa was staring fixedly at the wall. Luiz was slugging down the last of his whiskey. Claudia's lover, whatever the hell his name was, was pop-eyed with shock. Claudia, still standing beside him, was flushed with anticipation of what would happen next.

Well, she was going to be disappointed.

Rafe fixed a smile to his lips, walked towards Carin and took her hand.

"Ah, *querida*," he said, and pressed his mouth to her fingers, "I was beginning to wonder why you were delayed in joining us, but now I can see it was because you were making yourself even more exquisite than you already are." Carin's pupils contracted; he felt her hand jerk within his and he tightened his hold. "I've been telling our guests all about you."

Her eyes narrowed. Whatever reaction she'd expected, it wasn't this. Good, he thought savagely. Let her see that two could play at this game.

"Come, *querida*." He tucked her hand into the curve of his arm and drew her away from Claudia, towards the da Sousas, instinctively leaving what surely would be the best moment for last. "Isabela, this is Carin. My wife."

Isabela cleared her throat. "How nice to meet you, my dear."

"And this is Isabela's husband, Luiz."

Luiz da Sousa took Carin's hand and kissed it. "I am charmed."

Carin flushed. Isabela looked as if she'd stepped out of a Paris salon; her husband was a dead ringer for Paul Newman.

"Any friends of Rafe's are friends of mine," she said in the squeaky whisper that she'd thought so clever just moments ago.

Rafe put a hand in the small of her back. "And this is— my apologies, *senhor*. I'm afraid I've forgotten your name."

"Carlos Garcia, Dona Carin. *Muito gosto.*"

"I'm—I'm pleased to meet you, too, *senhor*," she stammered.

Was it possible…could she have made a mistake, tonight? Her appearance had achieved the effect she'd hoped for. The stunned looks on the faces of Rafe's guests, the shock in his eyes and then the way his face had reddened with embarrassment and anger…

But she hadn't expected him to make such a quick recovery, any more than she'd intended to make herself a spectacle for such sophisticated company. And who was that woman whose hand Rafe had been holding, the gorgeous blonde with the endless legs?

Rafe slipped his arm around her waist and flattened his hand on her hip. His guests would think it an affectionate gesture. In reality, his fingers pressed, hard, into her flesh.

"And now, my lovely wife, I want to introduce you to a special friend. A very old and dear friend." He turned her around, towards the blonde. "This," he said, his voice a dangerous purr, "is Claudia Suares."

Claudia was tall. She was a knockout and she wasn't wearing something long and feminine, she was wearing something that barely covered her thighs. Her smile could have sold toothpaste, automobiles, maybe even world peace.

She was the kind of female women hated on sight, Amanda would have said…and Amanda would have been right.

Carin swallowed hard. "Hello," she said, proving that it was possible to fold your lip over a purple-smudged incisor and still manage to speak.

"How charming," Claudia replied, in a voice as soft as a feather and as sweet as spun sugar. She looked up at Rafe and shot him that megawatt smile. "What a naughty boy you are, darling, to put the woman you married and the woman you were supposed to marry at the very same dinner table. Oh, aren't we going to have fun?"

It was not fun. Not at all.

Carin's plan, her clever, clever plan, lay dead and defeated as a collapsed balloon. She'd seen it start to expire the second she'd walked into the living room but Claudia's announcement had provided the *coup de grace*.

Everyone had laughed pleasantly at the little joke, and then Rafe had explained that he and Claudia had once been engaged.

"Things didn't work out," Claudia had added with a hot, private look at Rafe.

"No," Rafe had said smoothly. "But we still keep in touch."

"We do, indeed," Claudia had purred.

"Really," Carin had said, smiling her lip-folding smile while she tried to figure out what that all meant. What was "once"? Was it six months ago? Six years? Or was it six weeks? And what were the "things" that hadn't worked out, and what did it mean, that they still kept in touch?

For the very first time, it occurred to her that her husband might have been in another relationship before he'd felt obligated to marry her. Maybe their marriage was why "things" hadn't worked out for Rafe and Claudia.

From the start, she'd been so hung up on the life she was leaving behind, on how Rafe was turning her world upside down, that she'd never stopped to wonder about what she might be doing, to his.

He and Claudia certainly seemed—close. All those little looks. The smiles. The little strokes of Claudia's hand on Rafe's arm, his hand, his jacket...

Conversation swirled around her. No one seemed to expect her to participate, and she didn't. Eventually, mercifully, dinner finally ended. Carin thought that meant the evening had ended, too.

She was wrong.

"Nonsense, *querida*," Rafe said pleasantly, and slipped his arm around her in another of those death grips. "The night is young. Let's have coffee and brandy on the patio."

No, she thought, no, and hung back as the others filed from the dining room.

"Rafe? I—I think I'll go upstairs. Please tell your guests—"

"*Our* guests," he said, and he bent his head to hers, put his mouth to her ear, as if to murmur an endearment. "You will stay until I dismiss you or so help me God, *minha mulher*, you will regret it."

She believed him.

So she let him lead her out to the patio, pull out a chair for her as if he were the most solicitous of husbands.

Elena brought coffee. Carin poured it into tiny cups as translucent and delicate as eggshells, and Rafe poured brandy into crystal balloon glasses, and she wondered if anyone could possibly tell that she was dying inside, that this night of carefully-orchestrated revenge had boomeranged, that instead of humiliating her husband, she had humiliated herself...

And that her embarrassment wasn't half as agonizing as being forced to watch the intimate by-play between Rafe and the woman he'd really wanted for his wife.

Someone told a joke. Someone else laughed. Isabela, who was as kind as she was charming, spoke to her. Carin simply smiled, nodded, and hoped she looked as if she were listening.

She wasn't.

She was looking at Claudia and Rafe, at the dark head bent towards the fair one.

She saw the woman who had once been engaged to marry him add a teaspoon of sugar to his coffee before he could reach for the bowl, heard her finish his sentences for him. She listened to Claudia's low laugh as Rafe leaned closer and whispered to her. She watched lovers so taken with each other that they'd forgotten the rest of the world existed...and she suddenly understood why her husband hadn't demanded she share his bed.

Claudia was his mistress.

Carin shot to her feet. Her gown, that damnably ugly thing, brushed against the table. Her cup and saucer fell to the tile floor of the patio and shattered.

Everyone stopped talking, looked at the broken china, then at her. She knew she should apologize, or make some little joke about her clumsiness, but her tongue felt too thick for her mouth.

"Oh," Claudia said, "how awful. You've spilled coffee on your gown." The perfect pink mouth curled up at the corners. "I do hope you haven't ruined it, Carin. I can only imagine how difficult it would be to replace something so, ah, so unusual."

"Claudia," Isabela said sharply, and the man who was Claudia's escort threw her a harsh look. But Rafe, Rafe, who was trapped in a marriage to her instead of to the beautiful woman he really wanted, said nothing.

Tears blurred Carin's eyes. She gathered up her miserable

skirt and walked quickly from the patio. When she stepped inside the house, she began to run.

"Carin," Rafe shouted.

She heard him coming after her and she quickened her pace, stumbling on the bottom step as she raced for the bedroom.

"Carin," he yelled, "wait!"

Wait? She choked out a laugh. She was finished taking orders from Raphael Alvares, finished with this travesty of a marriage. She never wanted to speak to him again, see him again, listen to him again.

He couldn't keep her here, no matter what he threatened. She was taking Amy and leaving him, tonight.

Panting, breathless, she reached his bedroom and flung open the door. Let him get an attorney. Let him get a battery of attorneys. That was what she should have told him, from the beginning, but she'd been confused, exhausted, ashamed...

She cried out as Rafe's arms swept around her.

"No," she said fiercely, and beat her fists against the powerful hands locked at her waist, but he lifted her off her feet, carried her into the bedroom and kicked the door shut behind him.

"Damn you," she said, "damn you, Raphael Alvares!"

"Are you crazy?" He turned her in his arms, jerking his head back to avoid her flailing fists. "Carin!" He caught her wrists in one hand, captured her chin in the other. "Stop it!"

"I hate you," she sobbed. "Do you hear me, Rafe? I despise you."

"And for that reason, you set out to shame me in front of my guests?" His mouth twisted; he had to remind himself that she was only weeks out of the hospital so that he wouldn't give in to what he'd wanted to do earlier and shake her like a rag doll. "What pleasure did it give you, to embarrass me tonight?"

"Me? Embarrass you?" Carin struggled uselessly to free

herself. "What about what you did to me? Flaunting your—your mistress under my nose. Inviting your friends here, to see my humiliation."

"Don't talk like a little fool!"

"It doesn't matter. I'm leaving you, Rafe."

He let go of her, folded his arms and stared at her through narrowed eyes. "No, you are not."

"Oh, yes I am. It's bad enough you forced me into this marriage—"

"We have a child to consider, or are you so selfish that you still think only of yourself?"

"Don't you dare say such a thing to me! *I'm* selfish? I think only of myself?" Carin flung her hands on her hips as she raised her face to Rafe's. "I suppose I'm the one who walked out of that bedroom that night and never looked back, that *I'm* the one who demanded this marriage, who set down a bunch of stupid, egocentric rules—"

"You are selfish, not to see the necessity of giving a child two parents."

"And you," Carin said, stabbing her finger into his chest, "you would give her a father who has a wife, keeps a mistress, and doesn't give a damn who knows it."

Rafe caught hold of her wrist. "I do not keep a mistress."

"Oh, give me a break! Your mistress is right downstairs, laughing at how well the evening went."

Two stripes of color appeared on his cheeks. "Perhaps I should not have asked Claudia here tonight," he said stiffly.

"Do you think you could have kept her a secret? Even if you'd gone on being subtle, I'd have found out." Carin twisted her hand from his. "I don't care. I don't care if you have a hundred other women. A thousand. You can have as many wom—"

"If that is true," he said with a smug little smile, "then why are you so upset?"

"Are you dense, *senhor?* I'm upset because I don't enjoy being made a fool of in what is supposed to be my home."

Rafe sighed and ran his hand through his hair. "This *is* your home."

"Not for much longer."

"Carin." He cleared his throat. "I have already admitted I probably shouldn't have invited Claudia. I also should have told you about her."

Carin laughed. "That's charming. What for? Did you think I'd give you my blessing before you took her to bed?"

"You are my wife," Rafe said harshly. "You are the only woman I will take to my bed from now on."

"Oh, that's even better." She swung away from him, knotted her hands into fists until her nails bit into her palms. "Do you expect me to be flattered that you'd use me as a—a substitute for your lover?"

"You mean," he said, his voice taking on an edge, "as I was a substitute for yours?"

"Damn you, Rafe!" She spun towards him. "That's a lie! I slept with you because I wanted to, because you made me feel—you made me feel…"

She stared at him, her heart pounding, wishing there was a way to call back those foolish words. Time seemed to stop. Finally, she took a step back.

"Just—just let me go home." Her voice was a ragged whisper. "Let me take the baby and—"

Rafe's hands closed on her shoulders. "What did I make you feel, *querida?*"

Carin shook her head. "Nothing. I don't know why I said that." It was true, she didn't. She'd never let herself really think about what she'd felt that night or why she'd gone into Rafe's arms. And she didn't want to think about it now, not with him a breath away. "Rafe. Please, let's end this. We don't have a marriage, we have a—a sad little soap opera. You married me for Amy's sake, but she'll sense the truth as she gets older. She'll know—"

His arms closed around her. She flattened her hands on his

chest, tried to hold him at bay, but he gathered her to him, held her rigid body against his.

"Answer me, *minha esposa*. What did I make you feel, when you gave yourself to me?"

His eyes were dark, as dark as the night that held the quiet bedroom in its embrace. Trembling, she turned her face away, knowing it wasn't safe to look into those eyes, or to answer his question with anything but a lie.

"I felt—I felt nothing."

"Ah. Nothing. Of course, I should have known." Gently, he captured her chin and made her look up at him. "That was why you trembled then, as you are trembling now, why you came apart in my arms." He smiled and took his handkerchief from his pocket. "I wonder what would have happened, if you had looked like this the night we met." Gently, he wiped away all traces of the purple lipstick. "I like to think I would have seen past the ugly dress, *querida*, but the lipstick... I don't know."

It was impossible not to give a shaky laugh. "Oh, hell," she said, "what must your friends think?"

"I will tell them it is an old North American custom," he said solemnly. "I will say that a bride is supposed to come to her groom looking as unattractive as possible, that it is a test of his feelings for her, to see if he still wants her, even if she wears a dress the color of..." He ran the back of his hand over the ruffle at her throat. "What is this color? Does it have a name?"

"Hideous Green. And you've completely changed the subject. Is Claudia your lover?"

"*Não.*" Rafe's smile faded. "She is not."

"Is she your mistress?"

"No."

"What is she, then? Is there some special term in your language for the part she plays in your life?"

"It is the same as in yours. She is only a friend."

"An extremely friendly friend."

"Yes, well…" He shrugged his shoulders. "I apologize, *querida*. I never realized she does so much, ah, touching. And, as I said, I should have told you about her."

"But you were engaged to be married."

"It was a long time ago. Five years. More than that. And I was the one who ended it." He slid his hands down Carin's arms, clasped her wrists. "She is a spoiled girl, not a woman, *querida,* and she is no more faithful to a man today than she was then." He drew a deep breath. "I believe that when a man takes a woman as his wife, they are obligated to honor their marriage vows. One man, one woman. No one else."

"She still—she still wants you."

"She flirts with every man she knows…" Rafe expelled a breath. "Yes. I suppose it's true. I advise her on business affairs but perhaps it's time she sought advice from someone else."

"You don't have to give her up on my account," Carin said stiffly.

"I gave her up years ago, *querida.*" He smiled, lifted her hands to his lips and kissed them. "Besides, you are much more beautiful than she is."

"Do you really think I care about…" She hesitated. "Am I? Prettier than Claudia?"

He grinned. "Definitely—although it was a bit difficult to see tonight."

"You mean, you don't like this dress?" Carin lifted her chin. "Well, it was your fault. You had no right to order me to move into this room."

"I had every right." He softened his words by drawing her into his arms. "You are my wife."

Don't melt against him, she told herself, oh, don't…

"We are married, *amada.* Why should I lie to myself, or to you?" He kissed her mouth. "I want you. And you want me."

She looked up into his dark eyes and asked the question that had haunted her all these months.

"Why did you steal away from my bed that night?"

"You locked yourself in the bathroom." His tone hardened. "You made it clear I was no longer needed."

She sighed and laid her hands on his chest. "I only did that because—because I was ashamed of what I'd done."

"Sleeping with a stranger," he said quietly.

She nodded. "And—I'd been so—so wild..."

He groaned, gathered her against him and kissed her. She held back, but only for a heartbeat. This was her husband. She had the right to want him, to give herself to him, even if their marriage wasn't based on love. For the first time since the night they'd created Amy, Carin let herself melt into Rafe's arms.

"I've never forgotten that night," he said against her mouth. His voice was rough and low but his hands were gentle as they stroked down her back. "It was—it was like nothing I've ever known before."

She sighed and leaned back in his arms. "For me, too."

Rafe cupped her face and stroked his thumbs over the bones in her cheeks. "You are so beautiful," he whispered... Beautiful, and fragile, he thought, and frowned. She weighed nothing; he knew that from having carried her to the house earlier in the day. Now, he realized that the bones in her cheeks were pronounced. There were shadows under her eyes, too, dark as bruises. "You are exhausted, *querida,* and I am to blame. Your doctor tells you that you are well and what do I do? I invite half the world to dinner—"

She smiled. "Maybe not quite half the world."

"We should have spent the evening alone. I should have put you to bed hours ago."

"Put me to— Rafe? What are you doing?"

"What I should have done instead of tormenting you with Claudia." He had turned her so that her back was to him. Now, he was unhooking the awful ruffled neckline, pulling down the zipper of the dress. "I'm putting you to bed."

"No! I mean, I can do it myself..."

"Shh."

He bent forward as the gown slid from her shoulders and pressed his mouth to the nape of her neck. A soft moan rose in her throat and the sound of it, the knowledge that she wanted him and was no longer denying it, turned him as hard as stone.

But he would not make love to her tonight. She was exhausted, and it was his fault. She was hurt, too, and that, also, was his fault. He had forced her into a marriage instead of leading her into it, he'd stolen her from her own life.

He would make it up to her, starting now. He would not make love to her. It was true that he had waited for this night, but there would be others. Many others. He smiled, thinking of all the years that stretched ahead. He could build a life with this woman. They would share passion, share respect, share the love of their daughter.

He had never been foolish enough to believe in the kind of love that was supposed to exist between men and women. He knew there was no such thing, not after having been raised on his mother's sad, silly, sentimental stories…and on the reality of her life.

A successful marriage could be built on many things. Love did not have to be one of them.

Gently, slowly, he lowered the gown, eased it down Carin's hips, to her feet. She stepped out of her shoes and he kicked them away, his heart racing as he felt her tremble under his touch, felt her skin heating under his mouth and hands. He stroked his hand down her spine, spanned her waist with his hands, kissed her shoulders, and groaned with the pleasure of it. She tasted of honey and moonlight, of flowers and of desire.

Desire, for him.

Rafe took a deep breath. Then he turned her towards him and looked at her.

She was even lovelier than he'd remembered. Her breasts rose in creamy swells above a white lace bra; she wore tiny white lace panties and sheer white hose that clung to the tops of her thighs.

He whispered something in Portuguese, lifted a hand and ran it lightly over her breasts, watching her face as he touched her, as he stroked her belly, then slid his hand between her legs and cupped her.

She was hot and wet, and knowing how much she wanted him almost drove him to his knees.

"Do you like it when I touch you, *querida?*" he said softly.

"Yes." The word sighed from her throat. "Oh, yes, I—"

She cried out as he undid her bra. Her breasts tumbled into his waiting hands.

"Deus." He groaned, ran his thumbs over her nipples, his eyes hot on hers as her head fell back in a posture of total abandonment. "You are so beautiful, *minha esposa.* You steal my breath away."

"I—I gained weight," she whispered. "I thought—I wondered what you'd think, if you saw me. I wasn't sure—"

Rafe bent his head, kissed her breasts, licked the tightly puckered tips. He ached to kiss her thighs, to put his mouth at their apex and inhale her scent but he knew, if he did, he would come apart.

Instead, he stood up straight, kicked off his shoes, shrugged off his jacket and undressed, taking off everything but his black silk shorts.

Carin's gaze swept over him. She hadn't really seen him clearly the night they'd been together all those months ago. Things had moved too fast for that. Now, she could see the beauty of the man she had married. The hard, muscled shoulders and arms. The black, silky hair on his chest. The flat belly, narrow hips, long legs...

The heaviness of his erection, pushing against the black silk.

Heat swept through her like wildfire. She felt her knees

buckle. "Rafe," she whispered, swaying towards him, and he scooped her into his arms and carried her to the bed.

He drew back the covers, gently laid her back against the pillows. Then he came down on the bed beside her and gathered her into his arms. *Deus,* how he longed to strip away the last bit of lace that protected her from him. To part her legs and bury himself deep, deep inside her.

No, he told himself, no. Not tonight.

"Carin." He brushed her hair back from her hot face. "Do you realize that you have never slept with me?"

"But—but I did. Of course, I did. That night—"

"*Não, querida.* We did not sleep together. You left the bed, and my arms." He smiled, took her mouth in a lingering kiss. "Will you sleep with me, now? Truly sleep with me, I mean, nothing else. Will you curl up in my arms, close your eyes and give yourself over to sleep?"

Carin pressed her palms to either side of his face. "Rafe." Her voice trembled. "You're being very—very generous, but I—I can feel what you really want. I'm tired, yes, but you're my husband..."

He kissed her again, drew her close. "*Sim.* I *am* your husband, Carin. And I can wait."

My husband, Carin thought, as Rafe stroked his hands down her back, kissed her temples, her hair. Oh, my husband...

She sighed, closed her eyes, relaxed in his protective embrace.

Within moments, she was asleep.

CHAPTER NINE

CARIN had slept through the night. Rafe had not. How could a man sleep with a warm, sweet-smelling woman in his arms?

A woman who was his wife.

She lay with her head on his shoulder, her face inches from his, one hand splayed across his chest. As dawn touched the windows with soft, rosy light he rolled carefully to his side, still holding her to him.

He wanted to start the day by drinking in the sight of her beautiful face.

He smiled. Ah, but she was lovely. And a night's rest had done her good. She had awakened only once, stirred from sleep by instinct, he supposed, for he had surely not heard Amy crying.

"The baby's hungry," she'd murmured, and Rafe had taken her in his arms, carried her to the nursery and watched, his heart filled with tenderness, as she nursed their daughter.

"We've been giving Amy some formula feedings," the nanny had said softly. "You needn't worry about the morning, *senhor.*"

The woman had smiled, and Rafe had smiled, and then he'd lifted his wife again, carried her to their bed, held her as she sighed, curled against him with her head on his shoulder and fell asleep.

Yes, today, the shadows beneath her eyes were gone. She still seemed too thin but he knew how to fix that. From now on, they'd take all their meals together. He'd introduce her to the delicious foods of his childhood, not the sophisticated stuff he ate now but the rich, spicy dishes that kept a hungry belly filled. And he'd organize a *churrasco*. There was nothing quite like a Brazilian barbecue. He'd invite the da Sousas and everyone else he knew, ask them to bring their kids, and introduce his wife to people who would like her and make her feel welcome.

As for Claudia…when he spoke with her again, he would make it clear that it was time for her to find another financial advisor, that he was a married man, that he would tolerate no disrespect towards his wife, no matter how subtle, because Carin deserved his respect, and his loyalty, and, most of all, his lo…

Rafe caught his breath.

Carefully, he took Carin's hand from his chest, then drew his arm from beneath her shoulders. She gave a murmur of protest and reached for him in her sleep. Her hand curled around the nape of his neck and she sighed, moved closer and snuggled against him.

Time stopped.

He stared up at the ceiling, his mind a blank, the only sounds in the universe the tick of the wall clock and the soft murmur of Carin's breath.

What nonsense was this? There was no such thing as love. He hadn't ever deluded himself to think there was. Passion— lust—was an understandable emotion. A marriage could be built on it, so long as you added other things. Respect. Loyalty. Fidelity. Friendship.

He believed in those principles. His wife would, too. He would demand them of her. One man, one woman. No one else. He had told her that, last night. Lust was what had drawn them together. Principle was what would keep them together, when desire was gone.

Carin sighed again and burrowed closer to him, her breath warm on his throat. A fist seemed to close around his heart. He wanted to gather her against him again, kiss her awake and what was that, if not lust? He recognized the emotion; he had been with many women, over the years, he knew what it was to come awake with his blood hot, his body hard. It was only that this was different. He felt—he felt…

Rafe groaned, gave up thinking, and gathered his wife into his arms. He put his mouth to her temple, to her cheek; when she sighed he eased her onto her back, stroked her hair, gently kissed her lips.

She came awake slowly, whispering his name, and a pleasure so deep it shook his soul swept through him. It was his name she said, even before she was fully awake, his mouth she sought as she embraced him and drew his head down to hers, his kisses for which she hungered.

Her flesh was hot as flame against his. Hot and silken. He angled his mouth over hers, deepening the kiss, opening her to him with the tip of his tongue. She moaned softly, threaded her fingers into his hair and touched his tongue with her own.

Ai, Deus, she tasted of morning sunshine, of honey and cream, of all that he had remembered during the past endless months.

"Carin," he whispered, her name as sweet as her taste, "Carin, *amada, desejo-te.* I want you, sweetheart. I want you so badly that I ache."

Her eyes turned dark. She put her hand around the back of his head, drew his mouth to hers for a kiss that was all the answer he needed.

Rafe drew back, watched her face as he slid the blanket from her body, saw the way her lips parted and her breathing quickened as on that long-ago night. He saw the sudden leap of her blood in the hollow of her throat, the expansion of her pupils until they seemed to fill her eyes.

"You are beautiful, *querida,*" he said softly, and then he let his gaze move slowly over all the rest: the mauve-tipped breasts, the narrow waist, the softly rounded belly and the triangle of dark curls at the juncture of her thighs.

"Carin," he whispered, and he bent his head, kissed her mouth, drank in the taste of her as he slid his hand over her, cupping her breast, curving it along her hip, tracing the line of her thigh. Her soft sighs of pleasure mingled with his, her body melted against his, and he gave up trying to think because there was no way to think, not when she was in his arms.

Rafe kissed her throat and shoulder, the soft swell of her breasts. She moaned his name as his head dipped lower; when he tongued the swollen crests, she made a little sound of pleasure that was almost his undoing.

"Rafe," she whispered.

Her sigh became a groan as he kissed his way to her belly.

"You're even lovelier than you were, *amada*," he whispered.

It was true. She was. A fierce sense of need swept through him, to take her, possess her, make her his at last. He knelt above her, let his fingers seek the silky curls that guarded the core of her femininity, slid his hand between her thighs and cupped her.

She was hot against his palm, wet with wanting him, and it almost drove him over the edge. He told himself to go slowly. He was afraid of hurting her; he had never made love to a woman who'd given birth to a child only weeks before…who'd given birth to his child.

He whispered her name, told her how beautiful she was, how much he desired her, the soft words of Portuguese slipping from his tongue as he eased himself down her body. Gently, he pressed his mouth to her belly, then to those silky curls. She gave a startled cry as he spread her thighs, put his hands beneath her and lifted her to him.

Then he put his mouth to her.

Her cry rose into the silence of the room, not the cry of a woman in pain but of one in ecstasy. His world trembled; he groaned, lost in the taste of her, in the knowledge that she was ready for his possession. He kissed her, tongued her, and when she arched towards him and came against his mouth, he moved up over her, knelt between her thighs, entered her slowly, moved within her slowly, his concentration almost savage as he focused not on the pleasure, oh, *Deus,* the sweet, sweet pleasure of all that satin heat around him but, instead, on whatever shreds of self-control he had left, knowing he must not ride her hard, that he must not hurt her—

"Rafe," she said, and she lifted herself to him, impaled herself on him, and he lost everything, his control, his logic, himself, as he exploded within her.

He collapsed against her, breathing hard, spent, filled with a joy he had never before known. Carin held him close, whispered his name against his throat. He put his arms around her, murmured sweet nonsense words to her in Portuguese and in English, and kissed her.

They lay that way while time slipped past, heartbeats slowing, breath sighing, until Rafe realized that his full weight was pinning his wife, his delicate wife, his wife only weeks past childbirth, to the bed.

He cursed softly, started to roll off her, but she tightened her arms around him.

"Don't," she said unsteadily. "Please don't leave me."

He thought back to that night, how she had frozen beside him, how they had left each other, and he kissed her.

"I will never leave you again," he said, in a husky whisper. "But surely, *amada,* I am crushing you."

He felt her lips curve against his throat. "You aren't."

"*Sim,* I must be." He kissed her again, more slowly. Her mouth was softly swollen and he loved the way it clung to his. "You are so tiny…"

"Tiny?" She laughed softly, brought her hand to his face and stroked the damp, tousled hair back from his forehead. My husband, she thought, this is my husband. "I'm not 'tiny,' *senhor.*"

"Delicate, then." He rolled to his side, gathered her close, smiled into her eyes. "Delicate, and so beautiful it takes my breath away, to look at you."

A soft rosy hue flooded her cheeks. "And mine, to look at you."

Rafe grinned. "This is not a time to tell me I have taken a wife who can't tell a good-looking man from a big, ugly *gaucho*."

"Stop fishing for compliments." Carin ran the tip of her finger down Rafe's nose. "You're not big and ugly, and you're not a *gaucho*." She gave him a smug look. "I still remember my sixth grade geography. *Gaúchos* are cowboys."

"*Sim*," he said, and caught her finger gently between his teeth.

"And they're from Argentina, not Brazil."

"Are-zhen-*teen*-ah," he said, and smiled. "But here, in this part of Brazil, we speak of *gaúchos*, too, and of the *pampas*."

It was lovely, lying in Rafe's arms and talking this way, as if they'd always known each other. She shifted closer to him, only wanting to feel all of him against her, but the simple action changed things instantly. His smile tilted; she felt the quickening of his body and the hot, sweet quickening of her own.

"*Querida*." He took a deep breath, curved his hand around her cheek. She could see the sudden tension in his face. "*Esposa*, I think—I think we should get up now."

"Get up?"

"Yes." *Deus*, he could feel his muscles knotting. "You know. Take a shower. Have breakfast..."

"...Find out what happened to last night's guests."

Rafe laughed. "I suspect they gave up waiting for us, and..." He groaned. "Don't do that, *querida*."

"Do what?" she said softly, and moved, ever so slightly, again.

"The shower is best," he said quickly. "A long one, that is very, very cold..."

"I have a better idea," Carin whispered.

She reached between their bodies and closed her hand around his erection. He growled, rolled her beneath him, caught her hands and pinned them against the pillow on either side of her head.

"You play with fire," he said thickly.

"Yes," she whispered, dizzy with desire and with her power over him.

Rafe summoned up the last of his self-control. "I don't want to hurt you, *querida*."

"You could only hurt me by telling me you don't want us to make love again."

"I will never tell you that," he said softly. Slowly, his eyes never leaving her face, he eased himself into her. "Take me inside you, *esposa*. And look at me, as you do."

She opened her eyes. Rafe was all she could see. His wonderful face. His eyes. His mouth.

"Look at me, and say my name."

"Rafe," she whispered.

He moved, moved again.

"Say it, *minha esposa*."

"Rafe," she sobbed, as he filled her, "Rafe..."

"Who am I?" he said fiercely. "Tell me what I want to hear."

"You are my husband..."

Her words, and the arching of her body, tore him from reality. He thrust harder, deeper. Carin dug her fingers into his biceps and cried out. And just before Rafe let go of his carefully ordered, tightly controlled world, an emotion that had nothing to do with sex flashed like lightning through his head, and through his heart.

Carin awoke to a room filled with golden sunlight.

She was alone, but not in the way she had been on that night so many months before. Rafe's presence was still here, in the warmth of the sheet where he'd lain beside her, in the clean scent of him on his pillow as she gathered it in her arms.

Carin sighed, rolled onto her belly and closed her eyes.

What an incredible night it had been. They'd been so furious with each other…who could have imagined all that rage would dissolve and turn first to tenderness, and then to passion?

Her husband was a remarkable man.

She smiled, threw out her arms and let them flop across the mattress. Not just remarkable. He was also—he was also…

Carin buried her face in Rafe's pillow.

It was silly to blush when you were all alone but she was sure that was what she was doing, blushing a bright red from the top of her head to the soles of her feet. It was just that Rafe was the most wonderful lover. Sex, what little she'd experienced of it, had never been anything like this. Rafe had stroked her, kissed her, touched her everywhere. The last time, she'd refused to let go of him and when they'd fallen asleep, he was still inside her.

She smiled. She felt sated, boneless, ecstatically happy.

She felt—she felt loved.

Carin's smile faded. She turned over, drew the covers to her chin and stared blindly at the ceiling.

They'd *made* love. That didn't mean she *was* loved. Not that she wanted Rafe to love her. Why would she? They could have a perfectly good marriage without love…whatever "love" was.

Her mother had loved her father, once, and he'd loved her, but would two people who really "loved" each other have ended up hating each other, instead? Her stepfather professed to have loved all his wives… Yeah, right. Carin huffed out a breath. Jonas's definition of the word wasn't worth thinking about.

Okay. So Amanda and Nick were crazy about each other. Being in the same room with them could even be embarrassing, because you always had the feeling that as much as they were polite and gracious around other people, what they really wanted was to close the door and be alone.

It was like that with her stepbrothers and their wives, too, but none of that was love.

It was lust.

Carin got out of bed, grabbed the robe that lay at the foot of it, pulled it on and went into the bathroom.

And that was fine. "Lust" was what had brought Rafe into her life; it was what had sent them into each other's arms, last night. And if they were lucky, it would be what kept them together, that and their devotion to their little girl because yes, Rafe was right, Amy was entitled to a home with both a mother and a father.

She sighed as she did all the mundane morning things that were anchors to reality, then plucked a brush from the top of the shiny black marble vanity.

"Love" was what she thought she'd found with Frank.

I love you, Carin, he'd said, not just once but often. She'd never used those same words to him but she'd thought them, and look how that had turned out. Frank's idea of "love" had led him into another woman's arms. Hers had left her jilted, nursing a broken heart...

Her hand stilled. Slowly, she opened the bathroom door and walked back into the bedroom.

That wasn't the way it had been. She hadn't nursed a broken heart, only an angry one. She'd never loved Frank. If she had, she'd have wanted to spend the nights in his arms. She'd have felt a little rush of joy whenever she saw him. She'd have dreamed about him, longed for him, been angry at him, sometimes, but with a passion that made loving him all the sweeter.

And she'd have longed for his kisses, as she longed for Rafe's. She'd have sighed when he touched her, as she'd sighed all this morning. She'd have stood wrapped in his robe, as she was wrapped in Rafe's, and buried her face in the collar, and inhaled his scent and wished, oh, wished, that she were in his arms...

Carin lifted her head and stared blindly at the window. It

wasn't true. It couldn't be. What she felt for Rafe was—it was desire. It was respect, too, she could admit that, now, though she'd have denied it only yesterday. And she liked him. Why wouldn't she? He was intelligent, he was funny, he was generous...

But she didn't love him.

She didn't want to love him. Love was dangerous. It was uncertain. It made you vulnerable to the worst kind of pain...

"Bom dia, querida."

She swung around and saw Rafe in the doorway, a silver serving tray in his hands.

"Did I startle you?" Smiling, he elbowed the door shut and came towards her. "I thought you might be like me. I am not worth bothering with until I've had my morning coffee."

That wasn't true. He was very much worth bothering with. Her heart gave a quick, crazy thud. Rafe's hair was tousled; his jaw was shaded with early-morning stubble. He was wearing jeans, zipped but unbuttoned, and nothing else except that sexy, devastating smile...

"Don't look so worried, *querida*." He grinned, put the tray on a small table near the windows and sat down on one of the two love seats that faced it. Carin sat down opposite him. He poured two cups of coffee from a silver pot, got up, went to where she sat and handed her one. "I didn't make it myself," he said, sitting beside her, "Elena did."

"Oh."

Oh. She raised the cup to her lips and buried her groan of dismay within it. Was that the best she could muster, for morning conversation with her husband? With the man she'd fallen in love with? Except, of course, she hadn't. She couldn't possibly have...

The cup wobbled. She put it on the saucer, put both carefully on the table and gave him a smile she hoped was steadier than her hand.

"Well," she said brightly.

"Well," Rafe said, and smiled back at her.

"I, um, I have to check on Amy."

"I already did. Her nanny gave her a bottle, and now she is fast asleep."

"Oh."

"I said we would be in to see the baby at lunchtime."

"Lunchtime? But what will we do until…"

Carin's eyes met his. It would have been difficult enough, facing him without embarrassment this morning. She'd known that. After all, she'd never awakened in a man's bed before.

It was worse, now. It was impossible. She was scared, not of him but of herself. He could never know that she—that she thought she might love him. She'd never tell him, never let him suspect. You gave a man so much power over you, if you did that…

"Carin." He took her hand, laced his fingers through her. "What's the matter?"

Her lips felt bone-dry; she ran the tip of her tongue across them. "Nothing. I guess—I guess I just don't know what I'm supposed to do."

"You're supposed to just let me look at you, *esposa.*" He brought her hand to his lips, turned it over and kissed the palm. "You are so very beautiful. I came close to waking you, to tell you that."

She smiled unsteadily, tugged her hand back and put it in her lap.

"Thank you."

"Something is wrong," Rafe said quietly. "Are you feeling unwell?" His eyes darkened. "Did I hurt you, *querida?*"

"No! No, I'm fine. It's just… It's just that I'm not very good at this—this morning-after thing."

His face went blank. "Why not?"

"Well…" She took a steadying breath. "Because—because I never awakened in anyone's bed before."

He didn't speak for a long moment. Then he nodded, as

if she'd told him nothing more important than that it was going to rain.

"Didn't you?"

"No." She dropped her gaze, suddenly knowing she had to tell him this, that he had the right to know it, that she *wanted* him to know it, even if he didn't sound as if he gave a damn, she thought with a sudden flare of anger. She looked at him. "Frank was the only other man I've ever been with."

Rafe's expression remained unreadable. "I see."

She shot to her feet. "Am I boring you, Rafe? Because if I am—"

"Carin." He caught her wrist and stood up. She could see something in his eyes now, some little flash of light. "Why are you telling me this?"

"Actually, I'm beginning to wonder." Her chin lifted. "I had some silly idea you might be interested, that as my husband you'd want to know that I'm not—not promiscuous, that when it comes to sex—"

"Don't stop now," he said softly, with a little smile she couldn't read. "Not when it's just starting to get interesting."

Color rushed into her cheeks. "What I'm trying to tell you is that I never spent an entire night with Frank, and that sex with him wasn't—it wasn't ever—"

Her voice faded. Rafe drew her to him, put a finger under her chin and tilted her face up.

"We made love last night, *querida*. There's a difference."

The breath sighed from her lips. "Yes," she said softly, "yes, there is."

"For a minute there, I was afraid you were about to tell me that Frank had been a lover you would never forget."

"Is that what you…? No. Oh, no. That's not it, at all. What I was trying to tell you was—was…" She stopped, bit down on her lip, then flashed him a bright smile. "Sit down. Let me pour you some more coffee."

He nodded, then sat. She filled his cup and handed it to him. He was awash in coffee already but maybe, if he sat here long enough, he could figure out what in hell was going on. Carin had just told him she'd only been with one other man, and that it hadn't been as good with that man as it had been with him.

Why had she told him that? Not that it wasn't good, hearing it. She'd told him, very clearly, that the ghost that had hovered over their marriage had been put to rest. But if that were true, why did she look so unhappy?

Deus, would a man ever understand women?

What had happened, in the last two minutes? For that matter, what had happened since the last time they'd made love?

Love, he thought, and the cup shook a little in his hand. It was true, though. There was a difference between making love and having sex. What he'd felt, with her, had been... It had been different.

Stay with me, she'd whispered, that last time, *stay inside me, Rafe.*

He had. He'd wanted to stay inside her, forever. In her arms, in her heart.

The cup clattered against the saucer. Carefully, he put it down, then rose to his feet. "Well," he said briskly, "I think I'll shower."

Carin looked up and nodded. "I'll get dressed."

"Good." He cleared his throat. "And, uh, and then I'll, uh, I'll be riding out with some of my men."

She nodded again. "Of course."

"Yes." He walked slowly across the room, paused and turned to her. "There've been puma tracks near the south pasture. The question is, can I chase the cat off or will he have to be..."

"Rafe," she whispered, and the way she said his name told him everything he wanted to know.

"Querida," he said, and opened his arms.

She flew into them, he gathered her to his heart, and in that moment, he knew that his life had changed, forever.

CHAPTER TEN

CARIN sat cross-legged on a blanket spread over the grass. Amy lay beside her, her little arms and legs pumping as she stared, wide-eyed, at the sky.

"You see?" Rafe said proudly. "She is watching the clouds. Such concentration on that beautiful little face, *querida*. I can only wonder what she must be thinking."

His shadow fell over them both. Carin looked up and, as always, her heart gave a little leap at the sight of her husband, who'd been working with his horses. Wearing jeans, a sweatshirt and well-worn work boots, he was big, rugged and gorgeous.

"Hello," she said, and smiled.

Rafe smiled back at her. "Hello, *querida*." He bent down, brushed his mouth over hers. She raised her hand, curled it into his shirt and drew him closer for a longer, deeper kiss. "I need a shower," he whispered, against her mouth. "I am sweaty."

"Mmm." Carin smiled, pulled him towards her again for another kiss. "You are sexy, is what you are." She bit teasingly into his bottom lip. "I missed you."

Rafe grinned, folded his legs and sat down beside her. He took her hand, kissed the palm, then folded her fingers over the kiss.

"Of course, you missed me. I've been away from you for almost two hours."

"Such self-assurance, *senhor*."

He chuckled, cupped her chin in his hand and kissed her again, a long, lingering kiss that left her sighing.

"Suppose I told you that I know you missed me because

143

I missed you?'' he said softly, leaning his forehead against hers.

Carin smiled. "Are you telling me that?"

"You know that I am, *amada*. I missed you very much. In fact, I have strict orders from my men, that I'm not to come back to work this afternoon. They find it amusing that I don't seem able to keep my mind on my work."

"Strict orders from your men, huh?"

"Exactly." Rafe gave her a last, quick kiss, then turned to his daughter. "And how is our little girl today?" He lifted Amy from the blanket. A loopy smile spread over the baby's mouth. "Do you see that, *querida*? She knows her *papai* already. Just look at that big grin!"

Carin didn't have the heart to tell him that their baby's "grin" was probably her reaction to all the milk that had gone into her tummy half an hour before. On second thought, Rafe could be right.

What female wouldn't be happy, if he held her in his arms?

Such opposites, she thought, her smile softening as she watched him with his daughter. Rafe, so big and rugged; Amy, so tiny and delicate. And yet, already, you could tell she was his.

The baby's hair was black and silky, like her father's. Her eyes were changing from newborn navy blue to Rafe's soft gray.

Daddy's girl, Carin thought.

Sometimes, she shuddered when she realized how painfully close she'd come to keeping them apart, her daughter and her husband…and how terrifyingly close she'd come to not having him in her own life.

It was hard to believe how much things had changed in just a couple of months.

Her days were long, and happy. Rafe worked at his office in the mornings while she spent time with Amy or leaned over Elena's shoulder, in the kitchen, learning the delicious secrets of Brazilian cooking.

In the afternoons, Rafe took her riding and showed her all his favorite places: the small, forested glade where sunlight glittered like wildfire on the leaves; the narrow valley where, he said, he had once been almost certain he'd seen a jaguar; the emerald-green pool where they'd swum, naked, and made love on the grassy banks.

Sometimes, he'd tell her, apologetically, that he had to work.

"You work every morning," she'd said the first time, "in your office."

Yes, he'd replied, but, well, this was a different sort of work. There were water pumps to mend, horses to gentle, an outbuilding that needed a new roof.

Carin had assumed he meant to had to oversee the work but when she wandered down to the stables, it was Rafe she saw in the smallest paddock, holding his hand out to a horse that was blowing through its nostrils and tossing its head, just as it was Rafe she saw a day later, straddling the top beam on a windmill derrick to fix the pump mechanism.

When she asked him about it, he shrugged his shoulders and smiled.

"Honest work is good for a man, *querida*," he'd said. "It quiets the mind, lightens the spirit and eases the soul."

It also made magnificent muscles, she'd thought that night, as she watched her husband get ready for bed. And when, a long while later, he'd kissed her, drawn her against him so her head lay on his shoulder and her hand lay, spread, across his chest, she'd wondered how she'd ever fallen asleep any other way than this.

Watching him now as he held their baby, looking up occasionally to flash a smile at her, she suddenly thought, *I'm happy.*

It was true. She was happier than she'd been in her entire life, happy and content and—and deeply, heart-and-soul, in love.

There was no point in pretending, not to herself. She loved

Rafe, had loved him for a long time, maybe since that first night, when he'd rescued her from herself.

It didn't matter when it had happened. It was enough that it had, that the life she'd envisioned as a lonely penalty inflicted upon her by an arrogant stranger had become, instead, a life bright with joy.

Even the moments that might have once been tarnished, were bright.

Claudia had taken to dropping by. Rafe had kept his word; he'd told her to find a new financial advisor, but still, she came to see him. For coffee, she said; for a bit of advice not about money but about which new car to buy; for all kinds of different things. Rafe was invariably polite, though each time she left, he'd sigh and say he was going to tell her—

Tell her what? Carin would ask him, as she went into his arms. That she could no longer discuss problems with him?

"She doesn't bother me," she'd tell Rafe, and it was true, she didn't, because Rafe would make a point of keeping his arm around her while Claudia visited, of kissing her gently on the mouth so that even when he took Claudia into his office, Carin felt as if he were still with her, holding her close and making it clear that she was the only woman he wanted.

The only thing that could possibly have made her happier would have been if Rafe fell in love with her.

Sometimes—sometimes, she almost imagined that he had. There was something in the way he turned to her, when he wanted her, something in the way he looked at her...

"Querida?"

Carin looked up. Rafe had risen to his feet, holding Amy in the curve of his arm. He smiled, held out his hand and Carin took it and stood beside him.

"Shall we go inside?"

She nodded, and a feeling of such happiness swept through her that she felt her eyes fill.

"Carin?" Rafe pulled her close against him. "What's wrong, *amada?*"

I love you, she thought, I love you, and I'm happy...

"Nothing," she said, and smiled. "Nothing's wrong. I just—I think I must have gotten something in my eye."

"Ah. I'll bet I have a cure for that," he said, and kissed her. Together, with Amy gurgling softly in musical accompaniment, they strolled up the hill, to the house.

He said he would shower, as soon as they gave Amy to her nanny.

He would, but not alone.

"It seems such a waste of water," he murmured, once he and Carin were alone in their bedroom. Smiling, he reached for the hem of her T-shirt, drew it up over her head and tossed it aside. "Don't you agree, *querida?*"

Carin caught her breath as her husband ran his hands down her arms, then over her lace-covered breasts.

"Yes," she said softly, "I do."

His smile tilted. "You see?" He undid the front clasp of her bra, his eyes darkening when her breasts tumbled free. "I'm glad you're aware of such things." He bent to her, took the tip of one breast into his mouth as he caressed the other.

She trembled as he undid her jeans, slid them down her legs, then slipped her shoes from her feet.

"I can never get enough of you, *querida.*" He rose, held her at arm's length, let his eyes move slowly over her until she felt the heat of his gaze burning her skin. "And I still can't believe you belong to me."

"Such a sexist thing to say, *senhor,*" she whispered.

His smile was all male. "But you are happy to belong to me, *senhora,* are you not? To be my wife?"

"Yes." She smiled, too, and wondered if her heart were in her eyes when she looked at him. "Oh, yes, I am. Except..."

Rafe's smile tilted. "Except?"

"Except, you still have your clothes on."

He laughed softly. "As do you."

"I don't." She blushed, even though it was silly. "I'm still wearing my panties."

"Mmm. You are a delectable sight, in that scrap of lace."

"Well, I want you to be equally delectable," she said, and, her eyes locked to his, she put her hand on his fly, closed it over the hard, aroused flesh pulsing beneath the denim.

Rafe caught his breath, caught her hand, brought it to his lips. "Be careful," he growled, "or you'll have to pay the price."

Carin moved towards him, pressed her body against his and wrapped one arm around his neck.

"Make me pay," she whispered, and he swept her up into his arms.

He made love to her there, on the bed, his clothes scattered on the floor wherever they'd landed. He was right; he was sweaty, and she loved it. The male scent of him, mingled with the earthy scents of leather and grass, was like an aphrodisiac. She clasped his face with her hands, put her legs around his hips, took him as deep into her body as she could and when she came, seconds before he did, she cried out his name.

Afterwards, when he tried to roll off her, she wouldn't let him go.

"I am too heavy for you, *amada*," he said, but she shook her head.

"Stay here," she said softly, loving the feel of him, the weight of him, and wondering how, and when, to tell him that she loved him.

Did a woman wait for a man to say the words first? Maybe not in today's world, where the rules had all changed, but Rafe's world was different. He treated her as an equal, yet with a tender arrogance that made it clear he was male and she was female.

And she loved that arrogance, that—that macho. It was part of what made Rafe the man he was, part of what made her husband special...

Her husband.

Surely, that tilted the balance. A wife could turn to her husband, smile and say, "I thought you might like to know that I've fallen in love with you," and then he would say— he would say—

"Come and shower with me, *querida*."

Carin closed her eyes, then opened them again. "Only if you'll promise to wash my back," she said, and felt his body shake with laughter, because washing her back had gotten them into trouble in the shower many times before.

An hour later, they lay in bed again, hair still wet from the water.

Rafe put his arm around Carin and gathered her close.

"You grow more beautiful each day, *esposa*."

She smiled. "It's our baby who grows more beautiful each day."

Rafe pressed a kiss into her hair.

"*Sim.* She does. Our little girl is going to be as beautiful as her mother." He gave a dramatic sigh. "This means trouble for me."

"Trouble, for you?"

"Of course." He lifted his head from the pillow and kissed her. She felt his mouth curve into a smile against hers. "I suspect I will be the kind of father who subjects every boy she dates to interrogation. What are his intentions? What kind of car does he drive? Has he had any speeding tickets? Does he drink? Where is he taking my daughter? When will he bring her home?"

Carin laughed. "I've heard about fathers like you."

"Well, wasn't your father that way, when you began dating?"

"He wasn't there." Carin sighed and laid her hand over her husband's heart. "My parents had split up by then."

"I didn't know that."

"Mmm. Well, we've never really talked much, about how we grew up"

"No," he said, after a second, "no, we haven't. I'm surprised, Carin. Your parents were divorced, you were raised without a father... Surely, that should have made you more..."

His voice trailed away.

"Made me more what?" Carin propped her head on her hand and looked down at him.

"Amenable to marrying me."

"Amenable to being commanded to marry you, you mean."

She said it lightly, even meant it lightly, because how she'd come to marry him no longer mattered, but she felt Rafe stiffen.

"I had no choice."

A tiny bit of the happiness inside her began to drain away. "I know that's what you thought, at the time, but—"

"It is what I knew, what I still know." Rafe drew his arm out from under her. He sat up and swung his legs to the carpet. "How could a woman who grew up without a father have wished that same fate for her child?"

Carin sat up, too. She drew the sheet over her breasts. His voice had become cool and accusatory. Amazing, how vulnerable you could feel, if you were naked.

"It would have been a mistake for my parents to have stayed together."

"That's a very modern attitude and commendable, I am sure, in North American circles, but—"

"In North American circles?" Carin reached for the silk robe that lay across the foot of the bed. "What is that supposed to mean?"

"Does it really need interpretation?" Rafe stood up, went to the dressing room and pulled on a pair of white silk boxer shorts. "It takes two people to make a child, and two people to raise it."

"Not always. If the parents don't love each other—"

"Love is not necessary in a marriage," he said coolly. "If people are adults, they can reach an accommodation."

Love is not necessary. The words rang in her head. She felt as if she were shaking, deep inside.

"As we have, you mean."

Her voice was flat. Rafe could feel her eyes, boring into his back. She was angry, but why? He was the one who had the right to be angry. She'd grown up fatherless, as he had. She should have understood the immorality of trying to keep him from their child. Instead, she'd put up barriers against him, made him into a villain, a man who'd had to force her into doing the right thing.

Still, all of that was behind them. They were married. They were, much to his surprise, happy together. They liked the same things, enjoyed each other's company, enjoyed each other in bed. What more was required, save for his mother's blind certainty that love should have been everything?

It wasn't. His marriage was proof. Couldn't Carin see that for herself?

He took a breath, turned and faced her. She was pale, though her eyes glittered dangerously; he realized she was hurt, not angry, but why would she be hurt by anything he'd said, when she knew it was all the truth?

"Yes," he said. "As we have reached one. Our marriage is a success, isn't it?"

Carin didn't answer. He cleared his throat.

"Perhaps I should tell you that I grew up without a father, too."

"Did you."

Still, that flatness in her voice. Rafe pulled on a pair of jeans, drew a T-shirt over his head.

"Yes," he said, and ran his hands through his hair. "Perhaps we should discuss this."

"This?"

"You know. Our childhoods."

Carin folded her arms. "If you like."

Deus, what was he doing? He sounded like a robot, but he felt like a man who'd stepped onto a frozen pond only to discover the ice was far thinner than he'd thought. Be quiet, he told himself fiercely…but he couldn't seem to shut up.

"It might help you understand why it is so important to me that Amalia—that Amy—grow up with a father." He slid open the glass door that led to the terrace and stepped outside. Carin hesitated, then followed him. "I think of her that way, sometimes. As Amalia."

"My. You really do believe in running things." Carin smiled tightly. "You mentioned that before, but I didn't give my daughter a Brazilian name."

"It isn't Brazilian." He looked at her, then out across the ranch. "It's Italian. And you *did* give it to her."

"I named my baby 'Amy.'"

"Our baby. And it was a fortuitous choice, because my mother's name was Amalia."

That was the last thing she'd expected him to say. Carin stared at Rafe for a moment. Then she sat down in one of the white wicker chairs that were grouped on the terrace.

"You've never mentioned your mother," she said slowly.

"And you never mentioned your father." He turned to her, leaned back against the wall and cleared his throat. "My mother was a dancer."

"In Italy?"

He shook his head. "Her parents came here before she was born. No, she was Brazilian. She had dreams of dancing on the stage but…" He shrugged. "It didn't work out. So she danced in clubs, in Rio de Janeiro." He frowned, tucked his hands into his pockets. "That was where she met my father."

"What was he like?"

"He was a selfish, arrogant son of a bitch." Rafe's mouth twisted. "Once he knew my mother was pregnant, he abandoned her."

"Oh," Carin said softly.

"Yes, 'oh.'" Rafe took his hands from his pockets, folded his arms and leaned back against the terrace wall. "She tried to contact him—she loved him, you see. But he wanted nothing to do with her, or with the child she carried."

"Did your mother raise you alone?"

"Yes. And for the few years she lived, she told me, endlessly, how she loved the man who had fathered me, until I hated him as much as she loved him, for what was there to love in this man who had turned his back on us?" Rafe jerked his chin towards the pampas. "All of this was his."

"He changed his mind, then? I mean, he must have, if he left this place to you..."

Rafe gave a bitter laugh. "He left me nothing. He lost his wealth and died with empty pockets and with this ranch in ruins." He stood straight and looked at her, eyes flashing. "I bought the ranch with my sweat, created everything you see, turned his failure into my success..."

"Rafe." Carin got to her feet and went to him. She reached out her hand, hesitated, then laid it on his arm. His muscles were hard as steel beneath her palm. "Rafe, I'm so sorry..."

"Don't be." He jerked away from her. "I don't admire men who whine. I only told you that story because, sometimes, when I look at Amalia—at Amy—I think of what her life might have been, of what your life might have been—"

"No! I was much, much more fortunate than your mother. I had a career. Amy and I would have been fine."

"Not without a father for her, and a husband for you."

She wanted to shake him, for the arrogance of that remark. Instead, she told herself to remember how much life had hurt him.

"You might be right," she said softly. "I was much more fortunate than your mother that way, too. The man who gave me my baby is a good man. A decent man. He didn't turn his back on me. He married me."

"You make it sound like a sacrifice, *querida*."

She looked up, into his eyes, afraid to ask the question. "Wasn't it?"

"No. I'm glad I married you."

Her heart seemed to stop beating. Maybe she'd been wrong. Maybe he had married her for the wrong reasons, and now all those reasons had turned into the right ones.

"Are you?" she said, with a little smile.

"Of course. It was the right thing to do."

The right thing to do. She felt the swift, merciless sting of tears behind her eyes. *Stupid,* she told herself, *how stupid you are, Carin.*

"Does Claudia know? About your mother and father?"

"Claudia? What has she to do with this?"

"Just tell me if she knows."

Rafe nodded. "*Sim.* I told her when I—when I asked her to marry me. I thought it was important she know the truth."

"Ah. It was important your fiancée know the truth. But not me. Not your wife."

"Carin." He reached out his hand but she jerked away.

"And—and I suppose she knows you married me because it was the right thing to do?"

"I don't understand where you're going with this, *querida.*"

Carin took a deep breath. "You know," she said briskly, "I've been meaning to ask you if you'd stop calling me that."

"Stop calling you…"

"*Querida.*" She pulled her mouth into what she hoped was a smile. "It's so—so affected. I really find it annoying."

She saw his eyes go dark. Don't, she told herself, oh, don't, but it was as if someone else were inside her, a woman filled with rage and pain and hurt who was speaking, and she was helpless to control the things that woman said.

"You should have told me this sooner," he said coldly. "I would have been happy to oblige."

"Thank you. Now, if you'd just answer my question, about Claudia. Did you explain the circumstances of our marriage to her?"

"There was no need."

"But she knows we married after I'd had Amy."

"I suppose. Anyone who can count—"

"Yes, you're right. Anyone who can count." She took a deep breath. "Amazing, the way you said that. Frank used to say the same thing."

"Frank," Rafe said, and now it was his voice that was flat. He looked at her as if she'd lost her mind. Well, maybe she had. But her heart was breaking. Anyone who knew Rafe knew why he'd married her—especially Claudia.

"Frank," she said, with a quick smile. "You do remember him, don't you?"

"*Sim.*" A muscle ticked in Rafe's jaw. "I remember him well. What has he to do with this?"

"Oh, nothing. I just—I just remembered, we were lying in bed once, talking—you know, the way people talk after—after sex—and I mentioned someone we knew who'd suddenly decided to get married, and Frank counted off nine months on his fingers, and—" She cried out as Rafe's hands bit into her shoulders. "You're hurting me!"

"How dare you speak to me of what you and this—this man discussed in bed." He shook her, lowered his head so his eyes were level with hers. "Do you think I want to hear this? Have you no shame, or respect?"

"I don't know what you're so upset about. Frank is history." She paused. "He's more history than your sweet fiancée."

"Claudia?"

"Claudia. Who drops by, has coffee, telephones you a thousand times a day. Who you lock in your office, with you…"

Rafe said something sharp in Portuguese, lifted his hands from Carin's shoulders and stalked away.

"I don't understand what's happening here. Claudia is not in my life anymore."

"Neither is Frank."

He swung around, folded his arms, gave her a cold, searching look. "He is not in your life, but his name trips from your lips."

"Well, it's only natural. He was—he was very important to me. So—so, for instance, when you talk about how much you love soccer, and how much I have to learn about it, I think of—of Frank. I mean, he loved soccer…"

Frank wouldn't have known a soccer ball from a tennis ball, and she never thought about him any more than she'd ever lain in bed and discussed anything with him, but what did that matter? She was in love with her husband and he was in love with some antiquated code of honor—and, most probably, with the woman he still regretted not having married.

"I take it that you regret that you married me, and not your old lover."

"What a question. You didn't give me much choice, Rafe, remember?"

His mouth thinned. "I did the right—"

"If you say that one more time," she said, her voice trembling, "I'm going to—to throw something at you."

Rafe's face darkened. "Perhaps," he said carefully, "we've said more than we should have today."

She knew he was furious and that he was trying to control his temper, just as she knew it would be smart for her to do the same thing, but she was beyond caution or logic, twisting under the torment of knowing she'd stupidly fallen in love with a man who would never love her.

"Perhaps," she said, "we should have said it all sooner."

"Carin. I know this hasn't been easy for you. This change in your life, I mean…" He stopped, looked at her, waited for her to tell him he was wrong but she didn't. *Deus*, she didn't!

"You're right. It has. Living here, in the middle of nowhere, far from my home, my friends…" She choked back a sob, wishing she missed her home, her friends, wishing she hadn't come to love this place, or this man. "But you never stopped to think about that."

"I had no choice!"

"Don't shout at me, dammit!"

"I am not shouting," he roared. "I'm talking, and reminding you of what brought us to this point. This—this precious lover of yours abandoned you."

"So?"

"So, you were so distraught that you went to bed with me."

"No!"

"Ah. Forgive me for getting the details wrong. Perhaps you'll refresh my memory, *querida.* We met. You had nothing on your mind but the party and having as much fun as possible, so you tumbled into bed with the first man you laid eyes on."

"That's not true!"

"No? Well, then, let's try something else. We met. You were drunk. And, because you were drunk, going to bed with a stranger seemed like—"

She slapped him. He caught her wrist, twisted her arm behind her and pulled her against him. She could feel the race of his heart, smell the anger coming off him like heat rising from the earth after a summer storm.

"I was unhappy." Her voice trembled; she looked up at him through eyes bright with tears of defiance. "You know that."

"Unhappy enough to go to bed with the first man who asked you?"

"No! It wasn't like that. You know that, too. What happened with us—with you and me—was—it was different."

"Was it?"

"Yes," she said. "It was."

Rafe looked at her for a long moment, waiting for her to say more, to tell him that going to bed with him had been different because—because it *had* been different.

He felt his stomach knot.

Why had it been different? Was she going to speak of love? To say that she loved him, or that he loved her? No. There was no such emotion as "love." And if she spoke of it, told him that what had happened between them was love, he would tell her...he would tell her...

"How was it different?" he said, and hated the coldness of his voice and the way his heart was banging in his throat, but suddenly he knew her answer would be the most important one in his life. "Tell me," he said roughly, "how was making love with me different?"

Carin wrenched her hand from his. She stood straight and tall, her dreams lying like a shattered mirror at her feet.

"It was different," she said, because all she had left was her pride, and the lie that would allow her to keep it, "because you made me pregnant."

CHAPTER ELEVEN

PALE sunlight, too weak to give life to the autumn leaves, filtered through the trees in Central Park and barely penetrated the windows of the guest suite in Amanda's New York City penthouse.

The room, ordinarily bright and cheerful, seemed filled with gloom.

Amanda, who had just entered, stood in the doorway for a moment, watching Carin. Her sister was seated in a blue velvet armchair with Amy in her arms. She was nursing her—or trying to nurse her, with what appeared to be little success.

Amanda gently touched her own swollen belly. Then she fixed a smile to her lips, walked briskly into the room and switched on a lamp.

"It's dark as a dungeon in here," she said brightly. She went to the windows, drew the blue velvet drapes and turned on another lamp. "I swear, if this keeps up we're all going to need sunlamps."

She looked across the room at Carin, but she was devoting all her attention to Amy. The baby was fussing unhappily, nuzzling Carin's breast and making annoyed little cries. Carin looked as if she was certain she'd failed at being a mother.

Amanda watched for a while. If at first you don't succeed, she thought, and sighed, and decided to give it one more try.

"Carin?"

"Hmm?"

"Honey, why not try her on a bottle?"

"She had a bottle, this morning."

"Well, sure. But if you're having, uh, having trouble..."

159

"I am not having trouble. I'm just going through a phase where things are taking longer. It's perfectly normal."

"So is supplementing more of Amy's feedings with a bottle, or even switching entirely, if you have to. The book says—"

"I know what the book says." Carin shifted the baby in her arms. "I bought it, remember?"

"Well, sure, but..."

Carin looked up, eyes narrowed. Okay, Amanda told herself, okay, be diplomatic. Remember what Nick told you he does when he's dealing with a thickheaded government official. Say what needs saying, but do it with a smile.

"I mean, I know you know what the book says. I just, uh, I just think you might have skimmed over some stuff, you know? Or maybe misread—"

"I don't believe this." Carin glared at her sister. "You read one book on babies, your own isn't even born yet, and, poof, you're an expert?"

"Poof," Amanda said, trying to hang on to her patience, "I'm your sister. I love you. And I love my niece."

"So?"

"So, I think you should reconsider putting Amy on bottles. And that you should stop looking at me as if you'd like to murder me. You're stressed enough—"

"I am not stressed."

"—stressed enough, without getting ticked off at me."

"Ticked off? Do I sound 'ticked off'?"

"No," Amanda said sharply, "actually, you sound like a jerk." Oh, hell. So much for patience and diplomacy. Amanda lifted her eyes to the ceiling in a silent plea for composure. "Sweetie, I'm sorry. You're not a jerk. I am, for giving you such a hard time."

"No, you're not," Carin said, her voice wobbling. "You were right the first time. Come take the baby, will you?"

Amanda hurried across the room and took Amy in her arms. "That's my good girl," she cooed, but the baby was only interested in getting a meal. "Oh, sweetheart, Aunt Ammy can't help you…''

"Aunt Ammy?" Carin said, with a little smile.

Amanda looked up. "Well, I can't see a baby going around saying 'Aunt Amanda…' It's good to see you smile, Sis.''

"Yeah." Carin buttoned her blouse and got to her feet. "Okay," she said briskly, "let's go find the kitchen in this place and I'll get Amy a bottle.''

"What do you mean, find the kitchen?" Amanda looped her arm through Carin's. "It's right where it's supposed to be, downstairs, tucked in among the trillion other rooms.'' She grinned. "Would you believe this place is smaller than Nick's palace?''

"Would you believe you'd ever have seen anything bigger than Espada?''

Amanda smiled as the women traipsed down the stairs. "No. And I'd never have believed I'd end up living in a penthouse—''

"Don't forget that palace!''

Amanda laughed, handed the baby to Carin and set about preparing a bottle. "I'll never forget it. Nick made certain of that, when he had me locked away in the harem. The crazy things men will do, when they're in lo…'' She bit her lip. "Damn! Sorry about that.''

"About what?" Carin's smile was very bright. "I don't expect people to censor their conversation, just because I left Rafe. Nick did something nuts because he loved you, and he thought you didn't love him. So? Are you supposed to pretend it never happened, whenever you're talking to me?''

"Well, yes. While the wound's still fresh, anyway.''

"What wound?" Carin laughed. "Honestly, there is no wound. I told you everything, Amanda. 'Love' had nothing to do with my marriage. Rafe married me because of Amy, and he made it clear what a martyr he was, for having taken me as a wife.''

"Bastard," Amanda said, and took Amy from Carin's

arms. "Here you go, sweetie. Aunt Ammy has your supper, all nice and warm."

"Don't call him that," Carin said sharply.

"Call him what? A bastard? For goodness' sake, Carin, I'm only calling it as I see it. The man's a—"

"It's a horrible word."

"Well, he's a horrible—"

"I never said he was horrible, did I?"

"If he's such a saint, why are you going to divorce him?"

"I never said he was a saint, either. He's just—he's a man, that's all. Rafe is just—"

"Excuse me. *Senhora* Carin?"

Amy's nanny looked from Carin to Amanda, then back again. "I thought I would take Amy upstairs now, if that is all right with you."

Carin nodded. Gently, she took her daughter from Amanda's arms. The baby had fallen asleep with the nipple from the bottle in her mouth. Carin kissed the top of her head, then carefully handed her to the nanny.

"She's been a little fretful."

"*Sim, senhora.*"

"So, she might wake up. The way she used to, remember?"

"*Sim.*"

"If she does—"

"If she does," the nanny said politely, "I will call you at once."

Carin sighed. "Thank you, Teresa. *Obrigado.*"

Amanda waited until the nanny carried the baby from the kitchen. Then she smiled at Carin.

"Teresa seems very nice."

"Oh, she is."

"Capable, too."

"Definitely."

"Want some coffee?"

"Sure."

Amanda busied herself at the stove. Carin took the cream pitcher from the refrigerator, the sugar from the cupboard. Minutes later, the sisters sat across from each other, sipping their coffee.

"Good coffee."

"My only culinary talent." Amanda grinned. "The cook is very relaxed about taking her day off. She knows she has nothing to fear from me."

"Is she the same cook you had before?"

"Oh, sure. She's been with Nick a long time."

"Mmm." Carin drank some more coffee. "I remember those cookies you used to bake, when we were kids."

"And I remember how you used to talk about everything under the sun, rather than talk about whatever was upsetting you. Looks to me as if some things never change."

Carin flushed, put down her cup and folded her hands on the table. "Nothing is upsetting me."

"You left your husband."

"I left a man I never should have married."

"Yeah?"

"Yeah."

Amanda sighed. Carin rolled her eyes.

"And I," she said, "remember that you used to give that irritating little sigh anytime you were about to stick your nose into somebody else's business."

"Good," Amanda said. "Then, you won't be startled when I ask you the obvious question."

"I can't think of one obvious question, but ask whatever you want. Just don't expect an answer."

Amanda sat back and folded her arms. "If you never should have married him—"

"I shouldn't."

"Well, then, why did you?"

Carin laughed. She went to the stove, poured herself more coffee, held out the pot. Her sister shook her head.

"Too much caffeine for the little prince."

Carin smiled. "You might be carrying a princess," she said, knowing that her sister had opted not to know the sex of her baby in advance.

"This is a prince. Only a boy would act as if he were kicking around a soccer ball inside my— What? Oh, Carrie, what did I say?"

"Nothing." Carin sank down in her chair and shot a big smile at her sister. "Go on. You were saying...?"

"I was saying that you don't strike me as a woman who'd marry a man she didn't want to marry."

"Well, I did. But I finally smartened up and realized I wasn't going to let him ruin the rest of my—the rest of my—"

"Are you crying?"

"No." Tears trailed down Carin's face. "Why would I be crying?" she said, and buried her face in her hands.

"Carrie." Amanda went to Carin's side and put her arms around her. "Tell me what happened, please. How soon after the wedding did you realize it had been a mistake?"

"I knew it was a mistake the second I agreed to marry him."

"But I must have spoken to you a dozen times, while you were living on that ranch. At the beginning you sounded, well, sort of blah."

Carin looked up and laughed through her tears. "Is that a scientific diagnosis, doctor?"

"You know what I mean. You sounded flat. I figured you were having a little post-partum thing, you know?" She pulled a chair close to Carin's and sat down. "I thought about paying you a surprise visit but, after about a month—"

"Six weeks," Carin said, and dug a bunch of tissues from her pocket. "Six weeks, and one night..."

She blushed. Amanda looked at her and blushed, too.

"Okay," she said, and cleared her throat, "after six weeks and one night, you sounded—look, I know you'll tell me I'm crazy, but you sounded as if you'd never been happier."

"I'm a good actress."

"You're a terrible actress, the same as me. That's why Sam used to get all the Cinderella parts in those school plays, remember? You and I were always the wicked stepsisters."

"Yeah," Carin said, with a sad little laugh. "We had fewer lines to ruin."

"Exactly." Amanda raised an eyebrow at the soggy mass of paper in Carin's hand. She took it from her with two fingers, dumped it in the trash, pulled several sheets from the roll of paper towels over the sink and handed them to her sister. "Blow."

Carin blew, then wiped her eyes, then sighed. "All right. I was happy. Kind of."

"And?"

"And then I wasn't. And I left Rafe."

Amanda sat down again and took Carin's hand. "That's it? You were happy, then you weren't, and so you packed up and left?"

"Yes," Carin said, and she began to weep, this time as if her heart might break. "He doesn't love me," she sobbed.

"Well," Amanda said cautiously, "did he actually love you when he asked you to marry him?"

"He didn't 'ask' me, he blackmailed me. I'd never have agreed otherwise."

"Aha."

"Aha, what?"

"Aha, I was right. I told Nick something was fishy. I mean, Mom made it sound like this romantic adventure. The dashing Brazilian and the beautiful American met at Espada, had a passionate night, then continued their affair in New York…"

"We didn't. The passionate night at Espada was it. Rafe made up the rest to make it easier on Mom."

Amanda reached over and tucked her sister's hair behind her ear. "I figured it was something weird like that, that maybe you'd dreamed up a story to appease Mom's maternal sensibilities. You and I talked on the phone, we had lunch, and you never once mentioned that you were seeing anybody, much less Raphael Alvares.''

"He threatened he'd take Amy from me, if I didn't marry him.''

"What? How could he have done that?''

"He had papers. Legal documents. He said he had contacts…''

"The rat.''

"So, I had no choice. And for the next six weeks, we—we lived in a sort of armed truce. Separate rooms, separate lives. And then—and then something happened, and it changed, and I began to see that he wasn't the cold, insensitive man I'd thought he was, and—and I fell in love with him. I *thought* I fell in love with him, I mean, because I didn't. Why would a woman fall in love with a man who doesn't love her?''

"I don't know,'' Amanda said softly. "Suppose you try and tell me.''

"Sex,'' Carin said, her voice trembling. "It was sex, that's all.''

"If two people are really lucky, sex can be a wonderful affirmation of love.''

"Well, that wasn't it. It was just…'' Carin bit her lip. "All right,'' she whispered. "I did fall in love with him. I never believed I could love a man, the way I loved Rafe. But he didn't love me. He married me because of Amy. Only because of Amy.''

"You married him for the same reason.''

Carin slapped her hand on the table and shot to her feet. "Haven't you been listening? I married him because I had no choice. And I don't love him, not anymore. I hate Rafe. I despise him. I'll always despise him!''

"Wait,'' Amanda said, as Carin rushed from the room. "Carrie…''

"Let her go," Nick said softly. "She needs to be alone for a while."

Amanda turned around. Her husband was standing in the door that led to the dining room.

"It's a classic mess," he said, "isn't it?"

"Yes," she said, and then she went into his arms, kissed him, and wondered why it looked as if not one of the Brewster sisters could meet a man, fall in love, and live happily ever after without having to go through the torments of hell.

Carin sat curled in the blue velvet chair, feet up, arms wrapped around her knees, and stared out the window.

Night had captured the city. It was night back home, too, but it was different there. There were no streetlights at Rio de Ouro, no blaring horns. The sky would be black and scattered with stars; the rustle of the brush near the stables might be the only sound that drifted on the night wind. Back home...

Back home? What was she thinking? She *was* home. She was in New York. Rio Grande do Sul, with its gently rolling grasslands, its coastal mountain range, wasn't her home.

It was Rafe's.

Carin leaned her head back. She was tired, that was the problem. Drained, emotionally and physically. She'd only been back a week, or was it more? Monday? Tuesday? What day had she left ho—

Dammit. What was the matter with her?

"I *am* home," she said into the silence. Even Rafe had finally understood that she belonged in her world, not his. Otherwise, why would he have let her go?

She hadn't spent any time wondering if he would, after their quarrel. All she'd known was that she was going to leave him, that he couldn't stop her. What she'd felt for Rafe, all the love, had turned to hatred so bitter that she'd trembled with fury as she packed her things and Amy's.

She was almost done when she heard the front door slam. Her heart raced as she listened to Rafe pounding up the stairs.

I should have locked the door, she thought, but it was too late. He flung the door open and filled the doorway with his size and his anger.

"What do you think you're doing?" he demanded.

Carin's heart was still going crazy but she spoke calmly. "What does it look like I'm doing?" she said as she tossed a handful of clothing into a suitcase. "I'm leaving you."

Rafe kicked the door shut. "You are not leaving me," he roared.

"I am." She turned and looked at him. Rage was etched into his face, into the way he held himself. "And you'd better not try to stop me."

He strode towards her, every step a menace. She wanted to run but she made herself hold her ground and he reached past her and slammed down the top of the suitcase.

"You are my wife."

"Not for long," she said, and moved past him to the closet. "Once I'm home—"

"You *are* home."

"Once I'm in New York, I'm going to start divorce proceedings."

"I will not permit it."

She looked at him and laughed. "You will not permit it? Excuse me, *senhor,* but I don't need your permission to file for divorce."

"You will need it to get a divorce, and I will not give it."

"We'll see."

"Besides, this discussion is all academic. I am not going to allow you to leave this house."

"No?" She swung towards him, trembling with an anger that was almost palpable. "What will you do, Rafe? Lock me in my room? Chain me to a wall? I am leaving you. The sooner you understand that, the better."

He folded his arms, looked at her with eyes so cold they might have been ice.

"Very well, Leave. I don't want you, anyway."

"No," she said. "You never really did."

Rafe's eyes narrowed. "Do not tell me what I wanted, Carin."

"I'm just telling you the truth but you're right, none of that matters now. I'm leaving, and I'm taking my baby with me."

"You are not! Amalia is mine."

"Her name is Amy, and I'm the one who gave birth to her. She's going with me." She turned away from him, grabbed a handful of things from the nightstand, opened the suitcase and tossed them in. "I'm a citizen of the United States of America. So is Amy."

"Amalia is also a citizen of Brazil."

"I'm not going to debate this. Amy goes with me. If you try to prevent that, I'll call my embassy." She moved past him, yanked garments from where she'd left them, on a chair, and dumped them in the suitcase, too.

"Call whomever you like. This is Brazil, and you are my wife."

"This is the twenty-first century, and if you think I'd leave my daughter with a man who has no heart, you're crazy."

"I have a heart," he said.

Some quality in his voice made her look up, but his expression, the set of his shoulders, hadn't changed. He looked like a man carved from granite.

"You don't have one that works," she said coldly, as she closed and locked both suitcases. "Get out of my way, please. Teresa is getting Amy ready, and the plane should be here soon."

"What plane?"

"I phoned Nick. Your friend, Nicholas al Rashid." Her mouth curled in a tight smile. "Or maybe I should say, my brother-in-law. I don't know why it took me so long to re-alize he probably has even better 'contacts' than you do."

"You involved an outsider in this?"

"He's not an outsider. I just told you, he's family. I told Nick that I wanted to come home, and he said he'd send his plane. If I'm not on it, with Amy, he'll know you physically prevented me from leaving."

She didn't add that Nick had told her she sounded as if she'd lost her mind.

"Put Rafe on the phone," he'd kept saying, and she'd kept saying there was no reason for him to talk to Rafe, and finally Nick had given a heavy sigh and said, all right, he'd send the plane but he hoped she knew what she was doing.

"Is that what you really want?" Rafe said, with barely concealed disgust. "To turn this into a battle? A scandal that will involve everybody? A war, where there will be no win-ners?"

"I'll do whatever it takes to get my daughter away from you." Carin walked towards him, head high. "You make speeches about doing what's right. About obligation, and re-sponsibility. But you never speak about the things that really matter, the things I want my little girl to understand. Things like love."

"Love," he said, and his lip curled. "There is no such thing."

"No," she said after a moment, and tears filled her eyes. "No, not in you, there isn't. That's why I'm leaving you, and taking our baby with me."

They stared at each other in silence. Then she turned away, wrapped her arms around herself and stared at the window.

"I would be grateful," she said, as if she were talking to a stranger, "if you'd let me take Amy's nanny with me."

Rafe didn't answer. She swung towards him and, for a heartbeat, what she saw in his eyes almost made her run to him and take him in her arms, but then it was gone and she knew she had seen only what she longed to see, not reality.

"I will spend time with my daughter whenever I wish."

Carin let out her breath. He was going to let her go. "We'll work out the details."

"Whenever I wish," he repeated. "Do you understand, Carin? If you try to keep me from her—"

"I won't shut you out of Amy's life," she said quietly, "not because of your threats but because you were right about one thing. A child should have two parents, a mother and a father. And I know, in your own way, you love our baby." She took a breath. "I'll send you my address and phone number, once I'm settled. For now, I'll be staying with Nick and Amanda. Call whenever you want to see our little girl, and I'll make the arrangements."

"Arrangements?"

"Yes. So that you and I don't have to see each other." She'd come close, then, to losing her composure. "I don't ever want to see you again, Rafe," she'd said, and her voice had broken. "Not ever, do you understand?"

He'd said nothing, only looked at her as if he'd never seen her before. She'd turned her back to him, not wanting him to see the tears running down her face, waiting for the moment when she'd hear the door open, then shut, behind him.

Instead, she'd heard the whisper of his voice.

"Carin? Answer one question. This—this 'love' you talk so much about. Did you ever imagine you might feel it for me?"

She hadn't answered, couldn't answer, not without breaking down. After a while, she'd heard the sound she'd waited for as Rafe opened the door, stepped into the hall and out of her life.

Now, thinking back, Carin rose from the blue velvet chair, walked to the window, and rested her forehead against the pane.

"Oh, Rafe," she whispered, "Rafe, don't you know? I'll always love you. Always, as long as I live."

She began to cry. After a while, when she had no tears

left, she lay down on the bed and curled into a tight ball. When she finally fell asleep, it was from exhaustion; when she awakened, it was because she'd realized that she had a favor to ask of Nick.

One favor. One thing, Rafe would never have to know. One thing, that she owed not to him, but to the little boy he had once been...

To the man she had lost, but would always love.

CHAPTER TWELVE

NICHOLAS AL RASHID, who still bore the honorary titles of Lion of the Desert and Lord of the Realm even though there was no longer an imperial throne in his homeland, looked across the table at his guest and wished he also held the title of Mind Reader Extraordinary.

Then, perhaps, he'd know what his silent, glowering old friend was thinking.

Rafe had flown into Kennedy Airport an hour ago. Nick had picked him up and driven him here, to his club. If they'd exchanged a dozen words in all that time, it was a lot. And of those dozen words, at least ten had been Nick's. Rafe seemed capable solely of saying yes and no.

Just now, he was turning a cold stare on their waiter, who had begun describing the specials of the day. Somewhere between lobster tails and New York-cut sirloin, Rafe raised his head and gave the man the look Nick figured the Medusa had used to turn men into stone.

The waiter's speech faltered. Nick decided it was time to come to the rescue.

"Steak for me. Rafe? What about you? He'll have the steak, too," Nick said quickly. "Uh, make them both medium-rare, green salads, baked potatoes... Is that okay with you, Rafe?"

Rafe grunted. Nick took that as a yes, nodded at the waiter, added that they'd appreciate two bourbons, no ice, a little water—

"No water," Rafe said, which increased his vocabulary by a word. Well, Nick thought, that was progress.

The drinks arrived in record time. Nick almost grinned.

173

The waiter must have decided to take no chances. He lifted his glass. Rafe glowered at him, then lifted his.

"To friendship," Nick said.

Rafe nodded, tossed back most of the bourbon, looked around for the waiter and pointed at his glass.

Oh, hell, Nick thought. This was not good. Rafe was going to drink his lunch, maintain a stony silence, and he was on a mission to Find Answers. That was what his wife had told him to do. Actually, it was what he wanted to do, anyway.

"So," he said briskly, "how was your flight?"

Rafe looked at him as if he'd lost his mind. "Long," he growled. "The weather was clear, no diversions, twenty-eight-thousand feet all the way. Anything else you'd like to know?"

Nick sighed, shook his head and drank some of his bourbon. Better and better, but then, he hadn't actually expected Rafe to say much of anything. It was, he thought with another sigh, one of the major differences between men and women.

A man with a serious problem would keep it inside. A woman would talk and talk. And then, just to be sure, she'd talk some more.

"Talk" was what had been going on in his apartment all week. Not his. Carin's, and Amanda's. Endless, nonstop, talk.

They talked in the guest suite. In the kitchen. In the living room. They talked on the terrace, if the day wasn't too cool and then, for good measure, they talked at night in the library. His wife and his sister-in-law never stopped talking, unless he entered the room. Then they clamped their mouths shut and stared at him until he smiled nervously, muttered an apology, and backed out the door.

"What do you and Carin talk about?" he'd whispered to his wife one night, when they were in bed. He had taken to whispering; it seemed safer that way.

Amanda had shrugged. "This and that."

"Carin's unhappy?"

"Yes."

"Is there anything we can do?"

"No."

"There must be something."

"She says there isn't."

"Then—then what do you talk about? What do you say to each other, if she's not happy but she doesn't want us to do anything?"

"I told you," Amanda whispered back. "We talk about this and that."

"This and what?" he'd finally asked and Amanda had shushed him, put her lips to his ear and said, actually, there *was* something they could do. Something he could do, anyway.

Carin had a favor to ask him.

Nick finished his drink, checked Rafe's, and signaled the waiter to bring two more.

Maybe putting a buzz on wasn't such a bad idea.

The next morning, Carin told him what she wanted. He'd listened. Then he'd listened again, but the Something she wanted done made no more sense the second time around.

"Let me be sure I've got this," he'd said. "You want me to see if you can have Amy's named changed?"

"Yes."

"Just her given name, not her surname?" He'd looked helplessly from his sister-in-law to his wife. "Uh, you decided you don't like the name Amy? I mean, I think it's a beautiful…"

Carin had choked back a sob and he'd fallen silent under the lash of his wife's baleful glare.

"Sure," he'd said quickly, "I'll ask around, see what it takes." And then, like an idiot, he'd repeated that Amy was a fine name and he really didn't understand this…

Carin had burst into tears. His wife shot him an icy look, wrapped an arm around her sister and led her from the room.

Nick stabbed his fork into his salad.

He'd finally made sense out of the Something his sister-in-law wanted him to do. And it was sad, because it told him she didn't just want out of her marriage, she wanted out of anything to do with Rafe.

Did she really hate him enough to want to rename their child?

Nick looked at Rafe, who'd shoved his salad aside in favor of his drink. In his view, Rafe's plan—to get drunk—made a lot more sense. He pushed his salad aside, too, lifted his glass and smiled at his old friend. Rafe didn't smile back but he raised his glass and touched it to Nick's.

Both men took long, thirsty drinks. Nick put down his glass, took a deep breath, and dove into the silence.

"Okay, I've reached a decision."

Rafe looked at him.

"You can get plastered, if you want. But you can't murder the waiter. I don't think my diplomatic immunity would stretch far enough to cover that."

Rafe's brows drew together. "I am not in the mood for humor."

"Well, it's a damn good thing you told me that because up until now, I thought we were in for a couple of hours of laughs."

Rafe's brows knotted even more tightly. Then his lips moved in what might have been a smile.

"I'm sorry. I know I'm not very good company."

"Hey, man, why should you be different? Nobody's good company these days. Amanda slouches around as if I were the enemy just because I wear pants. And Carin behaves as if..." *Hell!* "Never mind. It must be the weather. This early fall is..."

"What about Carin?" Rafe was out of his chair, leaning across the table. "Is she ill?"

"No."

"The baby? Is she—"

"No! I mean, yes, Amy is fine. They're both fine. I just—I didn't mean to mention Carin, you know?"

Rafe sat down. "She is my wife," he said stiffly. "It's impossible not to mention her."

"Well, I just didn't want to—"

"If she were ill, I would want to know it." He picked up his glass, took a drink, put it down and looked at Nick. "Even if we aren't living together anymore, I would still want to..."

His voice trailed away. "Rafe?" Nick said softly, and this time, when Rafe looked up, Nick almost groaned. The angry scowl, the cold-eyed glower were gone. What he saw etched into his friend's face was pain.

"Oh, man," Nick muttered. He looked around for the waiter, made a scribbling gesture in the air. "Let's get out of here," he said, but Rafe was way ahead of him. He'd already tossed a bill on the table, shoved back his chair and headed for the door.

"I don't know why she left me."

Rafe and Nick were sitting on a bench in Central Park, with only a couple of pigeons to keep them company. It was an unseasonably cool, windy day. Nick was freezing but Rafe was talking, and Nick figured not even pneumonia was too big a price to pay for that.

"We were getting along well," Rafe said. "Not at first, perhaps, but that was to be expected."

"Well, sure. I mean, you'd only known each other a few months..."

"We knew each other one night." Rafe cleared his throat. "The story about having been together in New York was a lie."

"Ah." Interesting, he thought. Did Amanda know about that? "Why? So Marta wouldn't be too upset by the elopement?"

"It was no elopement," Rafe said heavily. "I forced Carin into marriage."

"You forced her?" Nick thought about the Brewster sisters. It was tough to imagine any man being able to force them into anything. "How?"

"I made threats. I said I'd take our daughter from her... Don't look at me like that, Nicholas! I did what I believed was right."

"Well, yeah. Making Amy legitimate was right, but if Carin didn't want to marry you..."

"It worked out." Rafe got to his feet. Nick followed, and they began walking towards the street. "Eventually, Carin came to see things my way."

"How'd you manage that?" Nick smiled. "I adore my wife but getting her to see things my way isn't always easy."

Rafe thought back to the night of the dinner party, the night he'd slept with his wife in his arms for the very first time, and how they'd made love the next morning.

"Things just did," he said stiffly. "And after that—after that, I was happy. I thought Carin was happy, too." His voice softened. "She seemed happy, I swear it. We laughed. We sat by the fire in the evenings. We went riding, and we watched our little girl grow..."

Nick nodded. "Sounds as if things were fine."

"Yes. I thought so, too. And then—"

"And then?"

Rafe sighed and tucked his hands into his pockets. "And then we had a quarrel."

"Rafe, look, people do that. Even Amanda and I have had a couple of arguments. Just last month, she was trying to convince me that we should paint the nursery a color she calls Butter Honey but trust me, man, it's more like Butter Rancid. I mean—"

"We quarreled, Nick." Rafe's voice was low. "It was a bad quarrel, and by the time it was over, I knew the truth."

"The truth?"

"My wife is still in love with the man who jilted her."

Nick stopped walking. "Frank?" He laughed. "No way."

"It's true. She loves him."

"Rafe, she doesn't. That occurred to me, too, so I asked Amanda." Nick shook his head emphatically. "Carin's not pining for Frank."

"She is." Rafe turned towards Nick. "She told me so."

Nick sighed. "Rafe, old buddy," he said, dropping his hands lightly on the other man's shoulders, "it's a hard lesson but if there's one thing married life has taught me, it's that what a woman says isn't always what she means."

Rafe's eyes darkened. "Are you calling my wife a liar?"

Hell, Nick thought, and tried again. "I'm calling you naive, if you really think women won't mislead us, if they think the issue calls for it."

"Perhaps. But this was different. I saw what I never hoped to see, that my wife..." Rafe drew a shuddering breath. "There's no point talking about it. Take my word for it. She loves him."

"So, you quarreled about Frank?"

"No."

"Well, what was it, then?"

"Nothing. Everything." Rafe hesitated. "It was confusing. She still loves this man but later, when I thought back on what had gone on..." His eyes met Nick's. "I think, perhaps, Carin wanted me to tell her that I loved her."

"That you..." Nick stared at his old friend. "Help me out here, okay? She left you because you didn't tell her you loved her?"

The men's eyes met. Rafe's face took on a ruddiness that had little to do with the chill in the air. He stuck his hands into his pockets and started walking.

"Right. I said it was confusing."

"Not really. I mean, it sounds simple, to me. Why didn't you just say it?"

"Because I don't!" Rafe came to a stop again and swung

towards Nick, his eyes almost black with anger. "Carin is a wonderful woman. She's beautiful and bright. She made me happier than I thought a man could be. Waking in the mornings, with her in my arms. Falling asleep with her curled against me at night. Just being with her..." He swallowed hard. "But love? Love is a nonsense word, used by people who believe in fairy tales. It deludes those who pretend to feel it. I know this, Nick, and yet you think I should have lied to my wife? That I should have said, 'I love you, *querida*,' just to keep her?"

Nick looked at Rafe for a few seconds before he spoke. "You're going to have to help me with this, Rafe," he said carefully. "I thought you told me that Carin is still in love with Frank."

"What if I did?"

"Well, why would she want you to say you love her, if she loves him?"

"I don't know."

"And how can you be upset about her being in love with another man if love means nothing to you?"

Rafe's jaw hardened. "It means something to her."

Nick whistled softly through his teeth. "It's an interesting puzzle. And it makes me wonder..."

"Wonder what?"

"If you'd said you loved her, just to make her happy..." He held up his hand before Rafe could speak. "Hear me out, okay? If you'd said you loved her, and if she'd said she loved you, too, you'd have said, what? That she didn't know what she was talking about?"

"*Sim.* Yes, that is what I would have said."

"Or maybe you'd have said she was lying."

Rafe moved fast, knotted his fingers into Nick's lapels and dragged him forward. "I told you before. My wife does not lie!"

A muscle knotted in Nick's jaw. "Take it easy," he said quietly.

Rafe stared at him. *"Santos Deus,"* he whispered. He let go of Nick's jacket and took a step back. "Forgive me. I'm sorry. I don't know what's the matter with me. I can't think straight. I bark at my housekeeper, my secretary…my men go out of their way to avoid me."

"And you don't know what's wrong with you?" Nick smiled. "Rafe, old buddy, you're in love."

"No! I told you, I don't believe in—"

"Neither do a lot of us, until we meet the right woman."

The men stood looking at each other for a long moment. Finally, Rafe gave an agonized groan.

"All right," he said, "it's true. I don't know how it happened, that I, of all men, should have fallen in love but, *Deus,* I love Carin. She is my heart, my soul, my life." He grasped Nick's arm, this time in desperation. "But what does it matter?" His voice roughened. "She doesn't love me. She loves this man—"

"Forget that. I told you, what they say isn't always what they mean."

"Then…" Rafe cleared his throat. "Then, you think there's a chance? That I can go to her, take her in my arms, tell her that I have been the worst kind of fool…?" He stared at Nick. "What is it? Why are you looking at me that way?"

"Rafe. Dammit, I'm sorry…"

"Tell me what you know, Nicholas."

"I think it's too late for a reconciliation. You see, Carin asked me to do a favor for her. To check on something, I supposed you'd call it a legality…" He took a breath. "I guess you chose your baby's name together, right?"

"For heaven's sake, what has Amy's name to do with this?"

"Well, it isn't Amy. Not anymore. That was the favor Carin wanted, to find out how to go about changing the baby's name, legally."

Rafe froze. "She cannot take my name from my daughter. It is on the birth certificate. She is Amy Alvares…"

"The Alvares is still there. It's the 'Amy' part that's gone."

"The Amy part?"

"Yeah. Carin changed it. Your little girl isn't named Amy Brewster Alvares anymore. She's Amalia... Rafe? Rafe, what the hell are you doing?"

But Rafe had already run across Fifth Avenue, to find his wife and tell her that he loved her.

It wasn't quite that easy.

Rafe paced the living room of the al Rashid penthouse, waiting to see if his wife would even agree to see him.

Nick had caught up to him as he'd raced out of Central Park, taken him upstairs, told Carin her husband was here and then he'd hustled a protesting Amanda into her coat and out the door.

"But, but, but," Amanda kept saying, casting little glances at Rafe that were not friendly, but finally Nick kissed his wife to silence.

"She'll be down," he'd hissed at Rafe, just before he'd closed the door.

All Rafe could do now was wait, and hope, and pray.

He paced the room, paced it some more. He went to the wall of glass that overlooked the park, stared at the terrace...

"Hello, Rafe."

He spun around and felt his heart stutter in his chest.

His wife was standing on the stairs, her hand on the banister. She was wearing jeans and a sweater; her hair was tousled and she had no makeup on her face. She was, in other words, incredibly beautiful...but the look in her eyes was bleak.

He took a couple of steps towards her. "Hello, Carin."

"Nick said you want to see me."

"I... Yes. Yes, I do."

She came down the rest of the steps, wrapped her arms

around herself as she had the night they'd quarreled—the night he'd lost the only thing in life that mattered to him.

"I realized you want to see Am—to see the baby, but she's asleep. If you come back tomorrow morning, say, around nine…"

"Of course, I want to see her. But I came to talk to you."

Carin unfolded her arms and tucked her hands into her pockets. She swept past him and he caught a whiff of her scent, a soft fragrance that he sometimes half imagined he could still catch, drifting lightly on the air in the bedroom they had shared.

"I told you the rules, Rafe. You're to call, before you—"

"You renamed our daughter."

Carin turned and looked at him. A flush rose in her cheeks; her lips trembled, and that was when he knew, when he was certain, she loved only him.

"Nick's an idiot," she said sharply. "Why did he tell you that?"

Rafe smiled as he walked towards her. "He thought it had some meaning, *querida*, that it meant you would never take me back into your life, and he wanted to warn me not to have hope that you would."

"Well, he was right. Don't have hope, Rafe. I'm not—"

"Why did you change it?"

"Why? For—for tradition. For—for respect. For…" She caught her breath as he stroked a hand over her cheek. "Please, don't do that."

"What? Don't do this? Touch you?" He threaded his hands into her hair, those dark, silky locks, cupped her face, lifted it to his. "You used to like me to touch you. To hold you, *amada*, do you remember?"

"I remember telling you not to come here unannounced." Her voice wobbled; she tried to pull away from him but he wouldn't let her. "And I remember telling you not to use words like that when they had no meaning for you."

"What words?" he whispered, and he bent to her and kissed her mouth.

"You know what words. *Querida. Amada.* They don't mean a damn."

"They mean that you own my heart, Carin." A smile curved his mouth. "But you have never said them to me. I have never heard you call me *querido* or *amado.*"

"Why would I? I don't love—"

"Yes," Rafe said gently, "you do. You love me." He took a deep breath. "And I love you."

"You're just saying that, because you—you want me to come back, so our daughter will grow up in your home."

"*Sim.* I want that, very much. But what I want the most, *querida,* is to spend the rest of my life proving my love to you. Carin." He paused, knowing that all the words he'd ever spoken, the ones that had helped him purchase his ranch, that had helped him leave behind, forever, the little boy from the slums of Rio, were not as important as the ones he would speak now. "Carin, I never understood what love was. I thought it was a dream for the weak, a game for those who played it. But I understand it now, *querida.* I believe in it because I love you, with everything I am, and if you truly leave me, I will be empty inside, forever."

A sob broke from Carin's throat. "Rafe," she whispered. "Oh, Rafe, my love…"

His arms closed around her; hers looped around his neck. Rafe kissed his wife again and again.

"Let's get Amy," he said softly.

"Amalia," Carin said, and smiled.

Rafe kissed her again. "And then, *querida,* we will go home."

Carin buried her face against her husband's throat as he swung her into his arms.

"*Sim, querido,*" she whispered. "Let's get our daughter, and then, please, take me home."

EPILOGUE

IN MID-AUTUMN, on an unusually warm Sunday, another wedding took place at Espada.

Carin and Rafe were married again. It had been Rafe's wish. He wanted, he said, to share his joy with family and friends.

She was radiant in white. She wore a gown with a low-cut bodice of French lace, held up by slender white silk straps; the skirt was a long, graceful sweep of white silk. Her dark hair was drawn back in a French twist, though soft tendrils curled at her ears and at the nape of her neck.

Rafe wore a black tux and a white pleated shirt, and all the guests sighed when they saw the way he smiled at his bride when she reached the altar bedecked with blue and white silk wisteria.

"Who gives this woman in matrimony?" the justice of the peace asked.

"I do," Jonas Baron said, and kissed his stepdaughter's cheek.

Marta, who was holding Amy in her arms and sitting in the first row of white chairs, clutched her husband's hand as he sat down next to her.

"Isn't she lovely?" she whispered.

"All my girls are lookers," Jonas said gruffly, and kissed his wife's cheek.

"Amanda," Marta said softly, "and now Carin..." She looked at the altar, at the slender, auburn-haired bridesmaid who was her third daughter, and sighed. "Everything would be perfect if Samantha would meet someone and fall in love."

"You women won't be happy until you have every danged man on the planet hog-tied," Jonas said.

Marta smiled. "Something like that," she whispered, and then she rose to her feet along with everyone else, tears shining in her eyes, as *Senhor* Raphael Eduardo Alvares took the beautiful *Senhora* Carin Alvares into his arms, and kissed her with all the love that had, for so many years, been locked away in his heart.

Harlequin truly does make any time special.... This year we are celebrating weddings in style!

A
Walk
Down
the Aisle

WEDDING CELEBRATION

To help us celebrate, we want you to tell us how wearing the Harlequin wedding gown will make your wedding day special. As the grand prize, Harlequin will offer one lucky bride the chance to **"Walk Down the Aisle" in the Harlequin wedding gown!**

There's more...

For her honeymoon, she and her groom will spend five nights at the **Hyatt Regency Maui.** As part of this five-night honeymoon at the hotel renowned for its romantic attractions, the couple will enjoy a candlelit dinner for two in Swan Court, a sunset sail on the hotel's catamaran, and duet spa treatments.

A HYATT RESORT AND SPA

Maui • Molokai • Lanai

To enter, please write, in, 250 words or less, how wearing the Harlequin wedding gown will make your wedding day special. The entry will be judged based on its emotionally compelling nature, its originality and creativity, and its sincerity. This contest is open to Canadian and U.S. residents only and to those who are 18 years of age and older. There is no purchase necessary to enter. Void where prohibited. See further contest rules attached. Please send your entry to:

Walk Down the Aisle Contest

In Canada	In U.S.A.
P.O. Box 637	P.O. Box 9076
Fort Erie, Ontario	3010 Walden Ave.
L2A 5X3	Buffalo, NY 14269-9076

You can also enter by visiting www.eHarlequin.com
Win the Harlequin wedding gown and the vacation of a lifetime!
The deadline for entries is October 1, 2001.

HARLEQUIN®
Makes any time special®

PHWDACONT1

HARLEQUIN WALK DOWN THE AISLE TO MAUI CONTEST 1197
OFFICIAL RULES
NO PURCHASE NECESSARY TO ENTER

1. To enter, follow directions published in the offer to which you are responding. Contest begins April 2, 2001, and ends on October 1, 2001. Method of entry may vary. Mailed entries must be postmarked by October 1, 2001, and received by October 8, 2001.

2. Contest entry may be, at times, presented via the Internet, but will be restricted solely to residents of certain geographic areas that are disclosed on the Web site. To enter via the Internet, if permissible, access the Harlequin Web site (www.eHarlequin.com) and follow the directions displayed online. Online entries must be received by 11:59 p.m. E.S.T. on October 1, 2001.

   In lieu of submitting an entry online, enter by mail by hand-printing (or typing) on an 8½" x 11" plain piece of paper, your name, address (including zip code), Contest number/name and in 250 words or fewer, why winning a Harlequin wedding dress would make your wedding day special. Mail via first-class mail to: Harlequin Walk Down the Aisle Contest 1197, (in the U.S.) P.O. Box 9076, 3010 Walden Avenue, Buffalo, NY 14269-9076, (in Canada) P.O. Box 637, Fort Erie, Ontario L2A 5X3, Canada.

   Limit one entry per person, household address and e-mail address. Online and/or mailed entries received from persons residing in geographic areas in which Internet entry is not permissible will be disqualified.

3. Contests will be judged by a panel of members of the Harlequin editorial, marketing and public relations staff based on the following criteria:

   * Originality and Creativity—50%
   * Emotionally Compelling—25%
   * Sincerity—25%

   In the event of a tie, duplicate prizes will be awarded. Decisions of the judges are final.

4. All entries become the property of Torstar Corp. and will not be returned. No responsibility is assumed for lost, late, illegible, incomplete, inaccurate, nondelivered or misdirected mail or misdirected e-mail, for technical, hardware or software failures of any kind, lost or unavailable network connections, or failed, incomplete, garbled or delayed computer transmission or any human error which may occur in the receipt or processing of the entries in this Contest.

5. Contest open only to residents of the U.S. (except Puerto Rico) and Canada, who are 18 years of age or older, and is void wherever prohibited by law; all applicable laws and regulations apply. Any litigation respecting the Provice of Quebec respecting the conduct or organization of a publicity contest may be submitted to the Régie des alcools, des courses et des jeux for a ruling. Any litigation respecting the awarding of a prize may be submitted to the Régie des alcools, des courses et des jeux only for the purpose of helping the parties reach a settlement. Employees and immediate family members of Torstar Corp. and D. L. Blair, Inc., their affiliates, subsidiaries and all other agencies, entities and persons connected with the use, marketing or conduct of this Contest are not eligible to enter. Taxes on prizes are the sole responsibility of winners. Acceptance of any prize offered constitutes permission to use winner's name, photograph or other likeness for the purposes of advertising, trade and promotion on behalf of Torstar Corp., its affiliates and subsidiaries without further compensation to the winner, unless prohibited by law.

6. Winners will be determined no later than November 15, 2001, and will be notified by mail. Winners will be required to sign and return an Affidavit of Eligibility form within 15 days after winner notification. Noncompliance within that time period may result in disqualification and an alternative winner may be selected. Winners of trip must execute a Release of Liability prior to ticketing and must possess required travel documents (e.g. passport, photo ID) where applicable. Trip must be completed by November 2002. No substitution of prize permitted by winner. Torstar Corp. and D. L. Blair, Inc., their parents, affiliates, and subsidiaries are not responsible for errors in printing or electronic presentation of Contest, entries and/or game pieces. In the event of printing or other errors which may result in unintended prize values or duplication of prizes, all affected game pieces or entries shall be null and void. If for any reason the Internet portion of the Contest is not capable of running as planned, including infection by computer virus, bugs, tampering, unauthorized intervention, fraud, technical failures, or any other causes beyond the control of Torstar Corp. which corrupt or affect the administration, secrecy, fairness, integrity or proper conduct of the Contest, Torstar Corp. reserves the right, at its sole discretion, to disqualify any individual who tampers with the entry process and to cancel, terminate, modify or suspend the Contest or the Internet portion thereof. In the event of a dispute regarding an online entry, the entry will be deemed submitted by the authorized holder of the e-mail account submitted at the time of entry. Authorized account holder is defined as the natural person who is assigned to an e-mail address by an Internet access provider, online service provider or other organization that is responsible for arranging e-mail address for the domain associated with the submitted e-mail address. **Purchase or acceptance of a product offer does not improve your chances of winning.**

7. Prizes: (1) Grand Prize—A Harlequin wedding dress (approximate retail value: $3,500) and a 5-night/6-day honeymoon trip to Maui, HI, including round-trip air transportation provided by Maui Visitors Bureau from Los Angeles International Airport (winner is responsible for transportation to and from Los Angeles International Airport) and a Harlequin Romance Package, including hotel accomodations (double occupancy) at the Hyatt Regency Maui Resort and Spa, dinner for (2) two at Swan Court, a sunset sail on Kiele V and a spa treatment for the winner (approximate retail value: $4,000); (5) Five runner-up prizes of a $1000 gift certificate to selected retail outlets to be determined by Sponsor (retail value $1000 ea.). Prizes consist of only those items listed as part of the prize. Limit one prize per person. All prizes are valued in U.S. currency.

8. For a list of winners (available after December 17, 2001) send a self-addressed, stamped envelope to: Harlequin Walk Down the Aisle Contest 1197 Winners, P.O. Box 4200 Blair, NE 68009-4200 or you may access the www.eHarlequin.com Web site through January 15, 2002.

Contest sponsored by Torstar Corp., P.O. Box 9042, Buffalo, NY 14269-9042, U.S.A.

PHWDACONT2

If you enjoyed what you just read,
then we've got an offer you can't resist!

Take 2 bestselling love stories FREE!

Plus get a FREE surprise gift!

Brimming with passion and sensuality,
this collection offers two full-length
Harlequin Temptation novels.

Full Bloom

by *New York Times* bestselling author

JAYNE
——— ANN ———
KRENTZ

Emily Ravenscroft has had enough! It's time she took her life back,
out of the hands of her domineering family and Jacob Stone, the
troubleshooter they've always employed to get her out of hot water.
The new Emily—vibrant and willful—doesn't need Jacob to rescue
her. She needs him to love her, against all odds.

And

Compromising Positions

a brand-new story from bestselling author

VICKY LEWIS
THOMPSON

Look for it on sale September 2001.